A Wylder Undertaking

by

Laura Strickland

The Wylder West

A Wylder Undertaking

Cover Art by *Tina Lynn Stout*

The Wild Rose Press, Inc.
PO Box 708
Adams Basin, NY 14410-0708
Visit us at www.thewildrosepress.com

Publishing History
First Edition, 2021
Trade Paperback ISBN 978-1-5092-3550-6
Digital ISBN 978-1-5092-3551-3

The Wylder West
Published in the United States of America

He backed off a half step, his gaze consuming the casket's contents. As corpses went, well—

This one sure was beautiful.

She lay on the padded interior of the casket—which was, indeed, covered with satin—like a princess in a bower. To be sure, she looked like nothing so much as the heroine of one of those tales Gus had heard when young, back in Scotland—the one, maybe, who could be wakened with a kiss.

Or no, the other one, who had skin like snow.

Pity and dismay gripped him in equal measures, that a lass so young and lovely should be lying dead, and without a mark upon her that he could see. He wondered madly if she'd been preserved, perhaps with the chemical called formaldehyde that they used back East.

Corruption had not yet set in. Her face, a perfect oval, appeared very pale, framed by coal-black hair, a mass of waves upon the satin. Her lashes, just as black, lay in perfect twin fans, as if drawn on. Her lips looked deep pink against such stark pallor.

In contrast to her beauty, the clothes she wore might have been those of a lad. A rough cotton shirt, plain brown vest, and a pair of britches concealed her from his eyes.

Britches, of all things. What woman ever went to her grave dressed in britches?

Praise for Laura Strickland

"The setting is vivid. The characters are three dimensional. The plot takes so many turns…this story will have you biting your nails to the last page."

~*Sandra Dailey, Author*

~*~

"Laura Strickland is an excellent writer. She really brings the setting and the characters alive, and I'd like to read more…. Laura Strickland is an author to watch."

~*Marilyn Baron, Author*

~*~

"The historical detail and storyline meshed well. The characters resonated with me, and I felt what they felt. This one definitely goes in the 'will read again' pile."

~*Cocktails and Books Review*

Dedication

To my senior editor, Nicole D'Arienzo,
for her continued faith in me

Laura Strickland's Other Books

Another book in The Wylder West series is by Laura Strickland: *A WALK ON THE WYLDER SIDE.*
She also has several series of her own:
Buffalo Steampunk Adventures
Currently at 8 books and counting

~

Fairy Tales Retold
Currently at 3 books and counting

~

Hearts of Caledonia, a Trilogy

~

Guardians of Sherwood, a Trilogy

~

Plus numerous Scottish heroes and heroines:
Devil Black
His Wicked Highland Ways
One Enchanted Scottish Knight
The Berserker's Bride
Honor Bound: A Highland Adventure
The Hiring Fair
Mrs. Claus and the Viking Ship
The Tenth Suitor
And other titles:
The White Gull
Forged by Love (sequel to *The White Gull*)
Words and Dreams (sequel to *Forged by Love*)
Stars in the Morning
Awake on Garland Street
Christmastime on Donner's Mountain
Devil's Food Ripple with a Cherry on Top
Ask Me

Chapter One

Town of Wylder, Wyoming Territory
September 1878

"Please, Mr. Wright. I'd like her to have the best coffin I can afford. My Betsy, she deserves that. You can't imagine how hard she worked out on that farm of ours."

John Cranston made his plea in a low, throbbing voice while standing with his battered hat in his hands. A humble man, thought Gus Wright, who heard him out—one who likely seldom asked for help.

Cranston blundered on after a glance at the children who stood in a line behind him, arranged in order of height, tallest to smallest. "I know I can't give Betsy what she had comin'. But I'd like the chil'ren to see their ma laid out proper, like. The last sight they'll have of her, so to speak."

Gus's expression did not change—it rarely did. As the sole undertaker operating in the town of Wylder, in the Wyoming Territory, he believed a certain gravity befitted his position. He'd perfected his somber mien some years ago, as an apprentice to the trade. It worked as a shield as well as a professional countenance.

He gestured to his shop just behind him, a small plank building perched at the edge of the dusty street. A number of plain, pine coffins stood propped against the outside wall—Gus's wares. He'd knocked them together himself, and offered them at a good price.

He spoke in his deep voice, and with faultless courtesy. "I'm sorry, Mr. Cranston. These are all I have to offer you, and nothing fancy, as you can see. If you want something nicer, you should see the carpenter over the way."

Cranston's face crumpled. To Gus's alarm, tears flooded his eyes.

"Can't afford nothin' like that, Mr. Wright. Heck, I'll be lucky to pay you for one of them plain ones. Got to keep these chil'ren fed. I just thought…maybe a bit o' carvin' on the lid or somethin'. She never had pretty things in this life. Didn't ask for none."

Gus's heart quivered in his chest. Folk in Wylder might question whether the undertaker had a heart beneath his tall, whipcord exterior. In truth, that organ was particularly soft, which explained why he guarded it so well.

He thought of the fancy casket being shipped in from Cedar Rapids that very morning. Curtis Randolph, who owned the lumber mill, had ordered it for his newly departed wife and hired Gus to fetch it. Was it fair one wife should have so much and one so little?

"I don't do a lot of carving," he told Cranston, "not a lot" equating to none at all. "But I suppose I could try and carve in one or two flowers there on the lid, over where her head will lie."

"Where her head will lie," Cranston repeated, like a vow. "And I'll pay you just as soon as ever I can." He stuck out his work-roughened hand.

Gus sighed. If he added up all the money he hadn't been proper paid for coffins, he'd be near as rich as

Randolph.

He shook Cranston's hand. "Will you pick up the coffin when it's ready? Or do you need it delivered?"

"Sure would help if you could find a way to bring it out to us, Mr. Wright." Meanwhile, as Gus knew, Betsy would likely lie in the family's parlor—if they had a parlor, that was. More likely, they had a two-room house with a loft for the chil'ren.

Gus's ears caught a wail from far down the rail line. Here on the south side of the tracks, the train lent noise, color, and urgency to his life. Passengers, supplies, and sometimes dead bodies came in on the train.

He had to collect that fancy casket promptly before the train moved off down the line to Laramie. Curtis Randolph wouldn't be very pleased if he didn't. And Gus needed the fee Randolph had promised him.

"I'll do my very best for ye," he told Cranston, a hint of his youth in Scotland coloring his speech as it tended to do in moments of agitation. He'd lived in America sixteen years, and in Wylder for the last three. But a man's roots, it seemed, continued to cling to a measure of their native soil.

Now he looked around for his assistant, Neddie. At thirteen—and small for his age—Ned reminded Gus far too much of himself when he'd first landed in Baltimore as a shy, bewildered lad, shivering in his shoes. Neddie, too, had been tossed up on a far shore here in Wylder. Pity had made Gus take him in.

Now, catching sight of Ned's dark head down the street, he gestured wildly. "Lad, bring the cart. We need to collect that cargo."

Ned nodded and hurried to obey. Gus could hear

the train approaching, slowing as the engineer sighted Wylder station. Great gouts of steam spewed up, and the loud huffing made it seem as if the train were alive. A fire-breathing dragon, maybe.

Deafening, in any case. He directed Ned with gestures to the rear of the train, and the cargo car. It took both of them to steer the unwieldy cart, which Gus had repaired so many times he'd become familiar with every inch of it.

"Wylder Station!" the conductor bellowed. Folks immediately began disembarking.

Gus straightened his coat in an unconscious gesture. He owned but two coats, both with tails, which befitted his position. Back when he worked for Silas Groat in Baltimore, appearance had been nine-tenths of the funeral game, as Groat told him again and again. Groat backed up any criticisms of Gus's appearance with a thrashing, which tended to plant it in a boy's mind.

Yes, early lessons ran deep.

Gus had never raised his hand to Neddie, and never would. He recalled all too well the feel of old Groat's hands, hard as wooden paddles and somehow the more terrible for what they routinely touched. Gus's spirit shrank from the idea of that just as his flesh shrank from the blows.

Funny how he'd grown accustomed to handling the dead now, and it no longer bothered him, though the respect old Groat had impressed upon him still lingered, along with the memories of the beatings.

"Let's leave the cart here," he told Ned, with a nod at the decrepit wagon. Damned thing was heavy, and the boy sweated in the early September sunshine.

They had to stand and wait till all the passengers were seen off the train—not so many in a small town like Wylder—and the conductor signaled to Gus.

"This cargo has to be for you, Undertaker."

He led Gus and Ned up into the cargo car, where lay boxes, bags of mail, and a huge rectangular something, covered by a blanket.

Leaning forward, Gus uncovered one corner of the object. A gleam of warm, polished chestnut met his gaze.

He whistled through his teeth.

"Bet you don't see many like that, do you?" the conductor asked. "Finest one I ever saw. The fellow who loaded it in Cedar Rapids covered it all up and insisted we handle it with care."

"That we shall," Gus assured him. "Here, Neddie, take an end."

Gus waited for the boy to position himself before attempting to shift the casket. Used to such work, he often moved his empty pine coffins by himself.

But this was no pine box and weighed far more than expected. With a grunt, he got his end off the floor. With the conductor's help on Ned's end, they shuffled it to the open door of the car.

"Don't want to cause any damage," Gus said then. He'd never touched a casket of this quality—hadn't been allowed to, back at Groat's. Just witness the great heft of it!

Ned said, "Maybe if we go out and slide it down."

"Aye, lad. Get the cart into position."

"I'm not paid to help you," the conductor announced, and fled. Gus leaped to the dusty ground and looked around. Catching sight of Buck Standish, co-owner of the livery across the way, he raised a hand.

"Mr. Standish, if I might impose on your good nature?"

Standish came loping over. A tall man with black hair now tied back in a neat tail, he had arrived in town as a gun-for-hire, just a few months back. He'd since laid his guns aside, but you wouldn't know it from the dangerous look of him.

Gus liked him, though. The livery was a neighbor, and Standish seemed like an honest man. Besides, everybody in Wylder came from *somewhere*.

"Mr. Wright." Buck nodded. "What can I do for you?"

"I wondered if you'd mind helping us load a piece of cargo on our cart. I fear it's a bit too heavy for the lad."

Buck peered into the gloom of the train car. "That's a coffin."

"A casket, sir. There is a vast difference."

When Standish glanced at him questioningly, he clarified, "Coffins are what I build. This is a work of art destined for the wife of Curtis Randolph."

"Wouldn't want to damage it, then."

"Just so."

"You hop up there and take that end. The boy and I will take this."

A cautious struggle ensued, watched from a distance by the conductor. By the time the casket rested on the cart, they were all sweating.

"Daaamn," Standish drew the word out, "that thing's heavy."

"I am very grateful for your assistance." Gus put out his hand. "If I can ever return the favor—"

"I sure hope not," Standish said, and hoofed it.

"Come on," Gus told Ned.

"Gonna be a hard push."

"It's not far."

Putting their backs into it, they pushed the cart to the stark wooden building labeled, quite simply, Undertaker.

"Now what?" asked Ned, breathless.

Gus had intended to take the casket inside and polish it up before hiring a wagon from the livery and driving it out to Randolph's homestead. He eyed the door, which he'd widened to admit coffins and loads of lumber.

"I think we can push it in."

The sides of the cart nearly scraped the doorway, before the relative cool of the interior embraced Gus. He dug in the pocket of his waistcoat for a penny and handed it to Ned.

"Go get yourself one of those biscuits you like so much, from the bakery."

Ned's eyes lit up. "You want one?"

Gus wouldn't mind, but he shook his head. Who ever heard of an undertaker munching on a biscuit while he worked?

Once Ned pelted off, Gus ran admiring hands across the top of the casket. The rich, chestnut finish put his workmanship to shame. He charged a dollar for one of his coffins. Folks who couldn't afford that just wrapped their loved ones in a sheet or blanket and planted them in the ground.

He could only imagine what this beauty had cost. Seized by a sudden desire to view the interior—for some of these fancy models came lined in satin—he thumbed the lid, only to discover it had been nailed down.

Probably to keep the lid from falling open during transport. Those nails would have to come out anyway, and better here than at Randolph's.

He selected his smallest pry bar and inserted it with delicacy under the lid. He couldn't afford any damage and, in this heat, Mrs. Randolph couldn't afford to wait for a replacement.

Six nails. He pried them up one by one with the utmost care. The lid was hinged—a lovely adaptation. He set his crowbar aside and propped it open.

All the breath promptly left his body in a wild rush.

No wonder the casket felt so heavy. It had a damned corpse inside.

Chapter Two

Well, that certainly wasn't right. Curtis Randolph had told Gus he'd ordered a first-quality casket for his wife. That's what he'd called it. Had there been some terrible error at the mortuary in Cedar Rapids?

They must have sent the wrong casket—that was it. There'd been a mix-up during loading, and they'd shipped one that was, well, occupied. By a young woman, of all things.

He backed off a half step, his gaze consuming the casket's contents. As corpses went, well—

This one sure was beautiful.

She lay on the padded interior of the casket—which was, indeed, covered with satin—like a princess in a bower. To be sure, she looked like nothing so much as the heroine of one of those tales Gus had heard when young, back in Scotland—the one, maybe, who could be wakened with a kiss.

Or no, the other one, who had skin like snow.

Pity and dismay gripped him in equal measures, that a lass so young and lovely should be lying dead, and without a mark upon her that he could see. He wondered madly if she'd been preserved, perhaps with the chemical called formaldehyde that they used back East.

Corruption had not yet set in. Her face, a perfect oval, appeared very pale, framed by coal-black hair, a mass of waves upon the satin. Her lashes, just as black, lay in perfect twin fans, as if drawn on. Her lips looked deep pink against such stark pallor.

In contrast to her beauty, the clothes she wore might have been those of a lad. A rough cotton shirt, plain brown vest, and a pair of britches concealed her from his eyes.

Britches, of all things. What woman ever went to her grave dressed in britches?

Gus narrowed his eyes and whispered under his breath, "Jesus." What was he to do now? Run and try to catch the conductor before the train left, tell him there'd been a terrible mistake?

Remove the corpse and tote the casket on out to Mr. Randolph's place?

Kiss the princess, and try to wake her?

Ah, he might have his peculiarities, but a propensity for kissing corpses didn't number among them. Not even corpses as beautiful as this one.

He supposed that, under the circumstances, he needed to lift her out of the casket and place her, temporarily at least, in one of his rough-hewn coffins. He'd send a message back with the train and make sure Mr. Randolph got his wife's casket.

Very carefully, he slid his hands beneath the corpse's hips and shoulders, and lifted. She wasn't all that heavy after all.

He swept her higher, and she opened her eyes.

Gus leaped back, dumping the corpse unceremoniously back onto her satin bed.

He was used to the movements of the dead. They tended to make all kinds of twitches and grimaces as their muscles tightened. Once or twice, yes, he'd seen them open their eyes.

Why this felt so different, he couldn't immediately say.

He crept back to the casket—one step, two. He looked at the corpse, and she looked back at him.

Her eyes were blue. Not an ordinary light blue, like his. Hers held the same deep hue he might behold in the sky just before the stars came out.

Heavenly. Definitely the loveliest pair of eyes he'd ever seen. On a corpse or elsewhere.

She blinked at him, the black lashes sweeping up and down. Her lips parted.

"Who are you?"

By Jiminy, it appeared she wasn't dead.

****

The man peering at Phoebe over the edge of the casket looked like a caricature, an exaggeration. He looked like a picture she might have doodled in an idle moment while searching for inspiration.

Tall and thin, he appeared to have been cobbled together with string, an imperfect assembly. He had a narrow face flanked by rather luxurious sideburns of downy brown. A nice enough face, if bony and with a slightly hooked blade of a nose. Thin lips expressed unhappiness, but his eyes…

Those looked kind. Soft blue, and narrowed at the moment between thick brown lashes, they invited her to trust him implicitly.

She couldn't see much of his hair, just a brown fringe that matched the sideburns, since he wore a most remarkable hat. Phoebe blinked at it, wondering if it might be the product of a mad dream.

It could have been a top hat, once long ago, before

it suffered much ill fortune. It still possessed a top hat's height, and added to the man's stature. But it had been patched and re-covered and added to so many times it now seemed a suggestion of a top hat more than anything else.

Mostly gray, with some blue and purple stitched in. The blue matched the man's eyes.

"Who are you?" she asked. "Where is Emil?"

"Emil?" He repeated the name as if he'd never heard its like. She supposed it was an unusual name.

The man wearing the hat had a very deep voice, one her mother would have called sonorous. The vibration of it danced along Phoebe's spine.

She sat up with considerable difficulty, stiff in every limb, and peered about her. "He was supposed to meet me, and get me out of this thing. He helped me while I was aboard the train, and at the stops along the way." Only, she was clearly no longer on the train, but in a plain wooden building—a larger version of a shed, perhaps, stocked with…by heaven, those looked like roughly built pine coffins.

"Am I in Laramie?"

"No, miss. This is Wylder. Laramie is farther down the rail line."

She fastened her gaze upon the tall man and asked again, "Who are you?"

He gave a slight bow which should have looked ludicrous but somehow did not. "Allow me to introduce myself. Angus Wright, undertaker."

Undertaker! Phoebe swore under her breath. Or maybe not quite under her breath, since the man's brown eyebrows flew up.

"My client ordered this casket for his wife's burial.

It wasn't supposed to arrive with an occupant."

"I see. Well, if you could just shut me back inside and ship me on to Laramie, I'll have the casket sent back. On second thought, I need to use your outhouse first. I'm afraid it's rather urgent."

"Uh—" He blinked at her. "I see."

"You do have an outhouse here, in—in Wylder?"

"Certainly. It's out back."

"I've been shut in here so long my back teeth are floating." She scrambled up and, heedless of her cramped limbs, launched herself from the casket, which lay on the back of a cart. "Emil did let me out at a place called Lodge Pole last night, after dark. He was there on the train with me."

"Miss, if I might ask—"

She gave him a searching look and held up her hand. Could she trust him? Did she have a choice?

"You can ask whatever you like, but please let me visit your outhouse first."

He ushered her through a rear door to another room, which sported a woodstove and a narrow bed, among a clutter of other furnishings. A second door led to a barren yard, seared by bright sunshine, at the back of which stood the required facility.

"The wee housie," he pronounced.

She dashed for it, wondering all the while whether it would stay over her head for the duration, since it leaned so drastically to one side. While using it, to enormous relief, she tried to figure out what had gone wrong with the plan.

Where was Emil? What on earth was she to do now? Yes, they'd always known their scheme could prove risky. The risk increased if Emil failed her—

something she had literally bet her life he wouldn't do.

The undertaker had no reason to help her. He might well turn her over to the nearest officer of the law. She'd better not trust him.

Except—he did have those kind eyes.

When she stepped out of the tiny, overheated facility, dizziness seized her. How long since she'd had anything to eat or drink? She swayed on her feet and raised a hand to her head.

The undertaker stepped out on his long, thin legs and took her arm. "Here, miss. Are you all right?"

"I really don't know."

"Lean on me."

She did. Beneath her fingers, his forearm felt unexpectedly strong.

They returned to the crowded back room, where he toed out a chair and eased her into it.

"Water?" she begged.

He poured some, from a stoneware pitcher, into a cracked mug. It went down Phoebe's dry throat like a draught from heaven.

"Now, then." The undertaker leaned against the wooden table and crossed his arms. He wore a long, dove-gray frock coat with tails, a dusty pair of trousers, and cracked leather boots so ancient it was hard to tell what color they'd originally been. "Who are you, and what were you doing in that casket?"

Phoebe gave him a searching look. No question, she stood—or rather, now sat—in considerable peril. She hadn't liked this plan from the first. Well, who would like the prospect of being shut into a casket, no matter how comfortable, for untold hours while the train rattled over miles of tracks and the heat built to intolerable proportions?

There had been moments when she thought she'd die in there, when air seemed so scarce she felt sure she must suffocate, and her heart fluttered in panic.

Back home in Cedar Rapids, when Emil Herzog loaded her up, he'd assured her there would be ample air. However, the casket—as she could attest—had been very well built, and the lid fitted without any gaps.

She struggled to remember the whole journey, and failed. Yes, Emil had been there from time to time and had let her out to refresh and relieve herself. But the last time must have been hours and hours ago.

Where was Emil now?

She didn't remember the final part of the journey, which made her think she must have lost consciousness at the end. Until this undertaker brought her round with a single touch.

"I have never heard of this town—Wylder." she said.

He frowned. "A small enough place, just west of Cheyenne."

She'd heard of Cheyenne, yes. Emil had mentioned it. But she didn't remember stopping there, and he'd said he couldn't free her from the casket till they reached Laramie. The casket—her refuge—must have been unloaded at the wrong town. Perhaps Emil had gone on to Laramie, which meant it would take time for him to discover the error and come back looking for her.

Meanwhile, she had no one upon whom to rely except this long drink of water standing in front of her, watching her with those careful eyes.

Could she trust him?

Probably not, though every instinct bade her do so.

Trust aside, might she persuade him to help her?

Possibly. All too aware of the gifts she'd been granted at birth, as well as her failings, she understood her appearance had a decided effect on members of the male sex. Take Emil, for example. Mother insisted a woman must use whatever she could to survive in the world. It made no great sin, and the end justified the means.

Phoebe found herself in a pickle—several simultaneous pickles—and if charm could keep her safe until Emil showed up, well…

This undertaker was a man, if a curious enough type of one.

She gave him her best smile, and widened her eyes. "Kind sir, I appear to be in most desperate need of rescue. Could I call upon you to assist me?"

Chapter Three

Rescue? Gus's eyebrows flew upward, and he stared at the young woman in consternation. He needed to start this day over. Too many things had already gone wrong. In fact, it seemed too likely he still lay abed and dreaming. Aye, surely he only imagined he'd got up, dressed, and gone out to retrieve that casket.

Because beautiful young women—however poorly dressed—did not arrive in said fancy caskets. And they certainly did not play the part of a damsel in distress, or throw themselves on his mercy.

For certain, she was very lovely. But her appearance seemed somehow beyond the reach of even his fevered imagination. Granted, he did dream from time to time of finding someone to love, a wife perhaps, to assist him with the business and chase away his loneliness.

But no, his dreams had never stretched to this. Nothing about this woman matched his imaginings, from her delicate hands to those amazing eyes.

He had to hold on to his composure, his aplomb, until he found out what kind of trouble she'd brought into his life.

Because she must be trouble.

"That casket was ordered by one of my customers," he told her. "How did you end up inside?"

She took another drink of water. Familiar as Gus

might be with the funeral business, he couldn't imagine spending any length of time inside a coffin. He didn't want to.

"It is a long story."

"Why don't you start by telling me your name?"

She hesitated even over that, and her eyes dilated. Leaning forward conspiratorially, she said, "I am not sure I should. You see, I am on the run."

Oh, shit. Just as he'd feared. In a calm voice that disguised his dismay, Gus said, "On the run, inside a casket."

"Yes. I was hidden there, you see."

"Hidden. By this Emil fellow."

"Indeed." Her face lit. "You are very clever."

And she flattered him, no doubt to get him onside. Did she think him a fool?

"Emil was on the train with me. During our journey, he would come from the passenger car, usually after dark, and free me. Perhaps—perhaps he is keeping away because he saw you collect the casket."

This could not be good, none of it. The last thing Gus needed—the very last thing—was trouble that would draw unwanted attention.

"Why are you on the run? From what?"

She leveled her gaze on him, as if trying to measure his thoughts or his temperament.

"You'd best tell me that much," he pressed, "or I'll go straight to the sheriff."

"Ah—" She reached out a hand to him. "Please, do not."

Gus shook his head. It was precisely what he should do. Go to Sheriff Hanson and dump the problem in his hands. Then, see about delivering the fancy casket to Mr. Randolph.

No question. Maybe if he went now, by the time he got back she'd be gone. Disappeared like a dream at sunrise.

"Give me one reason why I shouldn't."

"You are a gentleman. I can see that from your—your fine garb. You would not be so ungallant as to betray a lady."

Gus grunted noncommittally.

"Well, then—" She glanced around the room. "Do you own this business?"

"I do."

"Just getting off the ground, it would appear, and still rough around the edges."

"I've been here three years."

She looked shocked. "I see you are slow to turn a profit."

"Eh?"

"Help me, and I'll help you in turn."

His eyes narrowed. "What sort o' help?"

"Financial, of course. There is a fortune following me. I will promise you a cut, if you assist me now."

"A fortune. You like to spin stories, don't you?"

"This is no story."

Damned if it didn't seem like one. "How can there be a fortune following you?"

Again, she hesitated.

"Look," he said, "if you want my help, you're going to have to trust me."

She bit her lip, a gesture that sent an unexpected jolt through Gus, as her perfect little teeth closed on her equally perfect lower lip.

As a man of twenty-six years, he spent a lot of his

time *not* thinking about women, as despite all his wishing, he was in no position—financially, as she implied—to court anyone. It did him little good. Wylder boasted any number of attractive young women. The thoughts persistently crept in, and being face to face now with the loveliest woman he'd ever seen affected his control in a dire manner.

"You'll need to be honest wi' me," he told her flatly.

"Trust is difficult for me. I have been betrayed in the past. And maybe now, by Emil, whom I thought I could rely upon for—well, for anything."

"Is he your…beau?"

Her black lashes fell. "He would like to be."

"So the two of you are in it together, this trouble of yours."

The lashes came back up. She studied Gus's face as intently as if she tried to divine the contents of his mind or heart.

She sighed. "My name is Phoebe Corbet. I am on the run from Cedar Rapids, Iowa. There is a fortune in stolen jewels following me."

****

The instant the words left Phoebe's lips, she regretted them. She shouldn't have confessed it. But she couldn't figure any way around the fact that she needed this man's help. At the very least, she needed him to find Emil and to retrieve the jewels from the next train.

But despite his kind eyes—she did not believe him a cruel or violent man—his face proved surprisingly difficult to read. No matter what she said, he barely changed expression.

A man who guarded his thoughts, for some reason,

who kept a particular demeanor in place like a shield.

He spoke the truth, though. She would have to trust him, at least for the time being.

He should be tempted by the money. Most folks were, and God knew this business of his appeared quite humble.

"Phoebe Corbet," he repeated.

"And you say you are Angus Wright?"

"Aye." He gave another of those formal bows that made the tails of his coat flare out, and extended his hand—long, bony fingers reaching for hers.

She placed her hand in his and went immediately dizzy. She swayed in her chair.

"Oh." She raised the other hand to her head. "I seem to be a bit overcome. The strain, perhaps, of being shut into that casket for so long."

He released her fingers. "More water, perhaps?"

"There was very little air inside the casket," she told him as he poured from the pitcher again. "And during the day, temperatures climbed most drastically. I do not remember much of the last leg of the journey."

"No doubt you passed out. You were quite senseless when I opened the lid."

"I might have died." She fastened her gaze on him. Was he the sort of man to fancy himself chivalrous? Might she play upon that instinct? "If you had not collected the casket and opened it when you did—"

He crossed his arms upon his chest once more. "Someone would have opened it eventually, Miss Corbet."

"But you did it so promptly. Had I remained shut in there much longer, perhaps unloaded with the other cargo and left in the hot sun—"

He lifted his brows and nodded. "It does grow warm at midday. I would not give much for your chances."

"So you see, Mr. Wright, you might be considered my savior, the answer to my prayers."

His face tightened. He didn't like that. Maybe she could learn to read him, after all.

Fixing him with an appealing stare, she leaned forward. "If you could see your way clear to helping me—"

"First you must tell me why you're on the run. From what?"

He had a curious accent, this man. It lurked like an uninvited guest in his deep voice. Well, so did she have a faint accent, the product of being raised by French speakers, and of speaking that language with her mother, in private. Jasper, her stepfather, didn't speak French, and they could discuss him privately, even in his presence.

The thing was, this man's accent seemed to grow stronger when he became agitated.

"What would you say, Mr. Wright, if I told you I was a thief?"

He stared at her harder and said nothing at all. After a moment, he swept the incredible hat from his head and forced his fingers through his light brown hair, which, being very thick, fell into waves after.

Removing the hat made him look younger, and very unhappy.

"So that's what you are? A thief?" he demanded.

"It is a long story, and not the way it seems."

"What ha' you stolen?" An accent, most definitely. "These jewels you've been prating about?"

"I've taken only what belongs to me rightfully."

His eyes narrowed. "You've robbed a jewelry shop?"

"No, no." She waved her hand. "I took them from my stepfather, who is a jeweler in Cedar Rapids, as payment for my services. He cheated both me and my mother. When we found out about it, we hatched a scheme which we carried out with the help of Emil Herzog."

"So ye were out for revenge?"

She drew a breath. "No, Mr. Wright. I assure you, I am out for justice."

Chapter Four

Justice. It was a fine word, and one Gus had often contemplated in connection with his former master, Silas Groat. No man—undertaker or otherwise—should be allowed to treat his apprentices the way Groat did, and get away with it. For Gus hadn't been the only one kept under the man's thumb—or within reach of his fist.

For the small sum of paying off a lad's passage, he had impunity to treat that lad like a slave, for the duration of his indenture.

Gus sometimes dreamed of returning to Baltimore and, now that he was grown, exacting retribution. Only he could never return. He'd escaped and successfully disappeared into the West, where he'd better remain.

However, the idea did reverberate with him. Did this clever miss utter it merely for effect, to win his cooperation?

He gazed at her, wishing he could see beyond the flesh, past her undeniable beauty. "Nevertheless, you're a thief."

Her exquisite complexion flushed. "I am, with good reason."

Aye, he thought, there was always a reason. "And you'd like me to take part in your illegal activities."

For an instant, anger glinted in her eyes, before she held her hands out toward him in a gesture of appeal. "I ask you only to refrain from turning me over to the law. As I have said, I did have good cause for doing what I did."

An honorable thief, then. Still if Gus didn't believe people were sometimes justified in acting against the law, he'd never have ditched his debt to Groat.

"Look," he said, trying to quell his native sympathy, "my lad will be returning here soon."

She looked surprised. "You have a son?"

"No, he's my assistant. If you don't want him to see you—"

Too late. Gus heard Ned come running in and pause abruptly, perhaps looking at the open casket.

With another glare for Miss Corbet, Gus swiftly moved through to the shop, closing the door between it and the back room.

Sure enough, Ned stood peering into the interior of the casket, which still lay on the rough cart.

"You opened it."

Indeed, he had.

"It's right fancy inside, ain't it? We gonna take it out to Mr. Randolph's place?"

"Yes. Would you mind stepping over to the livery and asking them to hitch up a horse and wagon for us? I'll pay them just as soon as Mr. Randolph pays me."

"Sure. Here." Ned thrust a frosted biscuit at him. "Mrs. Standish at the bakery let me have two for the price of one. I saved it for you."

"Mrs. Standish is a kind woman."

"And she makes good biscuits."

"Thank you, Ned. Run and ask for that wagon. Then you can help me polish this up before we load it and go."

"Gonna be quite some job."

It would not be so heavy now.

Gus took a moment after Ned pelted off to grope for his composure. Maybe the beautiful young woman in his quarters had been a product of his fevered brain. Maybe she'd be gone when he stepped back in.

Only, she wasn't. Her slightly panicked gaze met him and hung on. She'd gone pale again, and didn't look particularly well.

"We haven't much time," he told her. "Leave now, before Ned returns. You can go out the back."

"Leave? And go where?"

"I don't know."

"Mr. Wright, I need your assistance. If you can help me find Emil—"

"I am sorry." His pity got the better of him. "I guess you can stay here and rest until Ned and I get back from delivering the casket. But you'll have to leave after that." He held out the biscuit in his hand. "You hungry?"

She eyed the biscuit on his palm before accepting it. "I am starving."

"Well, then, take what water and ease ye need. Just, be gone when I come back, aye?"

"Mr. Wright—"

"I'll not harm ye, but I'll not help ye either."

She bit her lip again.

Not waiting for a further answer, Gus let himself back into the shop, closing the door firmly behind him. He took up a cloth and began polishing the rich, chestnut finish on the casket.

He didn't like lying to Ned, something he strove never to do. Lies, in his opinion, tended to pile up, one upon another.

Assisting Miss Corbet would cause him to lie. For all he knew, she could be lying blatantly to him now. Anything, to gain his sympathy.

"Mr. Standish's bringing the wagon around." Suddenly Ned was back, his face bright. "Maybe he'll help us load this up again."

"Maybe so. Grab a cloth, Ned. Let's get it ready."

"Sure is fancy inside, isn't it, Gus?"

"Sure is."

"Never saw the like. Mrs. Randolph's going to her grave like a queen."

"She is, at that."

"Do you think it's comfortable in there? It looks comfortable."

"I can't say, lad." Gus cocked an ear at the back room. Not a sound to be heard. Had she already gone?

"But, Gus, why would anybody make the inside of a coffin all comfortable? Not like the corpse can enjoy it, is it?"

"True. But I expect it brings some comfort to the person buying the casket—thinking as how their loved one will lie in luxury for eternity."

"I guess. How much you think this thing cost?"

Gus hated to guess. "More than you or I could afford."

"How can Mr. Randolph afford it?"

"He bought stock in the railroad, remember, before it came through." It had allowed him to build a fine new home, and turn the lumber mill over to someone else to run.

It hadn't kept his wife alive though, had it?

"Good job," he told Ned at last. "Let's push this

outside, get it loaded up and delivered."

By the time he got back, or so he promised himself, Phoebe Corbet would be gone from his life.

****

Phoebe listened to their conversation, coming through the door from the shop beyond, while she ate her biscuit. Tender and buttery, with vanilla-flavored icing, it made her want a couple more.

Emil had brought her water to drink at his last visit, there in the boxcar, but no food. She'd barely been able to see him, because it was dark, but he'd helped her sit up in the casket and cautioned, "Do not drink too much or you will need to relieve yourself."

"Emil, I feel so cramped and dizzy. How much farther to Laramie?"

"Not far. We should be there tomorrow. I will try to reach you and let you out before the baggage is unloaded. It should not be a problem. I can free you while the passengers are disembarking."

It should not be a problem. Yet it clearly had been. What had gone wrong?

Because she wasn't in Laramie. A town called Wylder, so the tall undertaker said. A place of which she'd never even heard.

And where was Emil? Why had he failed to come and free her as promised? Had he gone on to Laramie without her?

If so, then he would come back, looking for her. She had to sit tight. But where?

Emil, as she knew, was more than a little bit enamored of her. He'd spoken of it to Mother, laid hints that after all this ended, when they'd achieved some wealth, Phoebe should marry him.

But Phoebe had observed the effects of a hasty marriage between her mother and stepfather. In her view, marriage could turn into servitude for a woman, if by another name.

Still, alarm fluttered in her stomach when she thought of Emil. She hoped nothing terrible had happened to him. She might have no desire to marry him, but he was a dear friend.

She remembered begging him, when he shut her into that casket the last time, "Please, do not nail the lid down. I hate that sound and—and if something goes wrong, I won't be able to get out."

"Dear Phoebe, nothing will go wrong."

Only, it had. And now here she sat with no one besides a reluctant undertaker for a champion, and no refuge except this rough, wooden dwelling.

If the undertaker refused to help her, what was she to do?

Chapter Five

The shop, with its carefully lettered sign over the door that read merely *Undertaker*, lay quiet and seemingly deserted when Gus and Ned returned. The sun beat down on the plain pine coffins propped up out front, and a few flies buzzed aimlessly.

Mr. Randolph had been pleased with his delivery. Gus had stayed to help his daughter settle his missus on the fine satin bed—never revealing by word or look that it had been previously occupied—and Randolph had paid what he owed. Gus had dropped the hired horse and wagon off at the livery and walked home.

Now he felt all at sixes and sevens—tired and hungry, and not at all sure what he'd find when he went inside. Surely Miss Phoebe Corbet would have had the sense to remove herself from the premises. Either that or he'd imagined her in the first place.

"Here, Ned." He fished in his pocket for some more coins. "Go get yourself some lunch."

Ned eyed him. "What about you? You comin'?"

Gus hesitated. He could murder a glass of whiskey right about now, but he didn't say so. "You run along. I'll make myself a sandwich later. Want to get a start on that carving I promised Mr. Cranston."

"All right."

Gus told the lad, "After you eat, why don't you go play with that new friend of yours, Andy Arkwright?

You've earned a wee bit of time off."

A broad smile bloomed across Ned's face. "All right."

Ned pelted off, and Gus stood for a moment, absorbing all that surrounded him—the hum of the flies, voices from the lumber yard over on the next street, and the whine of a saw. Music drifted from the direction of the Wylder County Social Club, and from the livery came the tang of horse manure.

Despite all that, this was home—or as close to one as he'd likely ever know.

He remembered his home back in Scotland, if only in a jumbled sort of way. He'd been nine when he left, and had turned ten during the crossing. Home to him meant hills shaggy with purple heather, rain, and cool mornings alive with mist.

Nothing had prepared him for America.

But enough of all that. He had to get Mrs. Cranston's coffin ready—for whatever he might or might not be, he kept his promises.

He walked through the wide doors and paused, listening again. Nothing. She must be gone. His rush of mingled relief and regret shocked him. Of course, it was best she'd taken her crazy story and gone—

He pushed through to the back room, and froze. Not gone, no, for there she sat at his little table, looking near as startled as he felt.

Their gazes met and held. For a full minute, Gus stopped breathing.

"Oh, it is you," Phoebe said. "When I heard someone come in, I did not know whether I should run or hide."

Gus should run as far and as fast as his legs would

take him. Run, just like he had from Baltimore, to save his life. At that moment, he knew it to the root of his soul.

"Miss Corbet," he began, "I have been thinking about your…situation. And my involvement in it. I'm afraid I have to insist you go."

"No." She clenched her hands, folded together atop his table. "You must let me stay, at least till I can discover what has happened to Emil. I will make it worth your while."

"This is no place for you. There's no room, for one thing. And I have my young lad to consider. If he sees you, well, I don't think we can keep him quiet."

She spread her hands in appeal. "I have nowhere else to go."

"Go on to Laramie. Your friend, Emil, is no doubt there."

"If so, he will come looking for me. If only you will allow me to stay till the next train arrives—"

"That won't be for days. Look, Miss Corbet, I'm very sorry, but—I'm not in a position to help you."

She scraped her chair back and got up. Gracefully, she moved around the table and approached him. She looked as small as a lad, barely more than Ned's height.

Reaching out, she seized one of his hands in both of hers. Her skin felt cool, there in the stuffy room, and soft against his calloused palm.

"Please, Mr. Wright. I have nowhere to go, no money for a room, or food. If only you will let me stay—"

Gus flushed with heat. He liked the sensation of her touching him. Hell, he liked looking at her. No question about that. And sure, he'd like to play the hero in her beautiful eyes. But, a practical man, he'd long outgrown fairy tales.

He shook his head. "What about Ned?"

She pondered that for a moment before her face brightened. "I am dressed like a boy, yes? I will pretend to be one, for your Ned."

Gus eyed her slowly, from her lovely face and dark curls downward. "Ye may be dressed like a boy. You're not all that convincing."

"Why ever not?"

Gus's gaze hovered at her bosom before jerking upward. "Your hair—"

"I can braid that up and push it under a cap. Do you have a cap I may borrow?" She examined his top hat in turn. "Something other than that fantastical chapeau?"

"Fantastical?"

"I have never seen its like. Only a man of imagination could wear such a hat." She squeezed his fingers between hers. "One who is willing to take a chance."

"Miss Corbet, there's no place for ye here. These are bachelor's quarters."

"I will make do. Just for a few days, till the next train comes and I can collect my cargo."

"The stolen contraband, you mean."

"Do not look at it that way. The value of those jewels is owed to me. And I promise you a cut."

"Which would make me culpable, just like you."

The warmth in her gaze faded. She released his hand. "You are right. I bring you only trouble."

A whole, whopping load of it.

"Listen, maybe this ruse of you playing at being a lad will work better elsewhere. There are a couple of boarding houses in town. Bundle up your hair and do your best. You can rest here till Ned returns, right? But then I need you gone."

"When will Ned return?"

"I gave him the afternoon off. So you have a couple hours to make yourself a plan."

"Yes, right." She drooped where she stood. "Thank you for that."

Gus nodded. "Now, I have some work to do, out in the shop."

"Yes? What sort of work?"

"I need to fancy up one of my pine coffins. It's important, so you stay back here and keep quiet in case somebody comes in."

"Do people often come to your shop?"

"Some days, it's dead." A wry smile curled his lips. "Other days, you'd be surprised. No telling when somebody will get shot, in Wylder."

"I see. Business must, at times, be brisk."

"I wouldn't call it that. We get by, Ned and me."

"How do you intend to 'fancy up' this coffin?"

"I thought about a bit of carving on the lid." Gus stirred uneasily. He was no hand at detail work. "There's this small farmer, see, who just lost his wife. He'd like to lay her to rest in something pretty, but I don't think he can pay me."

Her expression softened. "Still, you are willing to try. I think you are a good man, Mr. Wright."

Gus shrugged. "Doesn't seem fair, does it, that one man can order up a fine casket for his wife, and another has to lay his in a plain pine box?"

"And you believe in fairness, do you?"

"I do, even though there's little enough of it in the

world."

She reached up and began fiddling with her hair, her fingers moving swiftly as she plaited it in a tight braid. "I think I have a solution for you."

"Eh?"

"First, find me a cap. Is there one here?"

"Just an old one of Ned's. It's pretty ratty."

"It will do. Then, do you have any paint?"

"Paint?"

"If not, please go purchase some."

"What kind of paint?"

"Pretty colors. I am thinking yellow, green and blue."

"What—"

"I am an artist, you see." She thumbed herself in the chest. "I will prove myself useful and make a coffin of which your farmer may be proud."

"Well, uh—"

"Go, go." She made a shooing motion. "Get me my paint. And I think—I think you'd best start calling me Phil."

"'Twill never work. You're far too beautiful to pass for a lad."

Again, they stared at one another for several moments, while heat stained Gus's skin.

Phoebe tipped her head once more. "Is that a compliment, Mr. Wright?"

"It's a caution. This is a mad scheme."

She leaned toward him and widened her eyes. "Sometimes mad schemes are the very best kind."

So said the woman who'd arrived in a casket, supposedly followed by a fortune in jewels.

She shooed him away again. "Go, go."

Gus went, fearing his hard-won life was no longer completely his own.

Chapter Six

The undertaker stood at the center of the shop, motionless as a corpse, and watched every move Phoebe made. Back in Cedar Rapids, she'd hated it when anyone watched her paint, especially Jasper, who always made her feel so uncomfortable.

But she didn't mind the company of Gus Wright. His presence felt reassuring, in fact. He both amused and intrigued her. He seemed so grave and rigid, even predictable. Then there was that hat...no predictable man would ever place such an object upon his head.

She thought about how he looked without it, all that thick, light brown hair, falling over his forehead. Not what she'd deem a handsome man, he nevertheless possessed a definite, if peculiar, attraction. And he had, without rival, the kindest eyes she'd ever seen.

She dipped her brush into the tin of crimson paint and applied it carefully to the pine coffin lid. He'd done very well procuring the paint at the local shop, or wherever he'd gone. He'd brought what colors he could—green, blue and not yellow but the crimson, as well as two small brushes.

Phoebe, an artist to her soul, had let her imagination run wild. Inspired by the red paint, she'd created a wreath of red and blue flowers twined together, forming a heart above the place where the poor farmer's wife would rest her head for eternity.

She happened to agree with Gus Wright that the farmer's wife deserved a pretty coffin as much as the rich magnate's wife did. Love was love, and should be honored. Anyway, she hated money with all its attendant power.

She hadn't done what she'd done—stolen a fortune in jewels—for wealth, but for justice, as she'd said to Angus. And to pay Jasper back for his ill-treatment of her and Mother. She knew all too well, however, that for most folks, money proved a powerful motivator.

Though not, apparently, for Gus Wright. And that made her like—and possibly respect—him. Other than her late father, she didn't respect many men.

Now Angus Wright watched, spellbound, as she finished the heart and scattered stray flowers across the bottom of the lid. She wondered if he was breathing.

She'd been crawling over the coffin lid for perhaps an hour. Now she rose to her feet and examined the work.

"Enough?" she asked him.

He cleared his throat. His voice came in a rusty rumble. "It's perfect. Perfect."

He pronounced the word *pairfect*, and she pondered where he must be from. Scotland, most likely, with a moniker like Angus. Emotion tended to thicken his accent—just like her mother. She and Phoebe, lately, had taken to speaking French more often than not, so Jasper couldn't eavesdrop on them.

She glanced at Angus. "You think it's all right, then?"

"I have no words. You certainly are a fine artist, Miss Corbet. To create such a vision on a plain, pine lid—"

She pursed her lips. The surface had been rough, not easy to work on. But the design looked bright, and pretty.

"So have I proved useful to you?"

Consternation flooded his eyes. As if in answer to her unspoken desire, he once more swept the top hat from his head and ran his fingers through his hair before slapping the hat back on.

"Aye. It is bonny."

Most certainly Scotland.

"Then will you let me stay?"

He fixed her with those kind and rather shrewd blue eyes. "I think you should travel on to Laramie. Your friend will quite likely be there."

"And I think I should stay put, so when he comes looking, he can find me."

"See here, Miss Corbet, I am not the proper man to help you."

"I think you are exactly the proper man. Who would suspect another lad you've taken in? And you'll be at liberty to check the cargo on the next train. You need only say you're expecting another delivery."

He looked unhappy. "Let me ponder that while I deliver Mr. Cranston's coffin out to his wee bit farm. On the way back, I'll stop and get us some supper. The lady at Jake's will wrap it up for me. She often does."

"I must admit, I am very hungry." Phoebe wondered if the lady at Jake's was sweet on this man. She wouldn't be surprised.

"You stay out of sight while I'm gone, mind."

"I will."

Very carefully, he loaded the pine coffin into his cart and laid the lid atop it with profound gentleness.

From the shadowed doorway, Phoebe asked, "Where is this farm?"

"Not far outside town."

"You're not intending to push the cart all that way? Why not hire the wagon again?"

"I cannot afford it," he said simply. "And I'm no' so weedy as I look."

"Soon," she told him, "you will be able to buy a wagon, if you like."

****

The sun beat down on Gus's top hat as he went, and sweat trickled between his shoulder blades. He thought about what Miss Corbet had said. Just imagine being able to buy whatever he needed. A horse and cart of his own. Maybe he could enlarge his quarters on the back of the shop. The idea was seductive, almost as much so as Miss Corbet herself.

A narrow, dusty trail led to John Cranston's house. Gus plodded up it, pushing the cart, and the kids, who played outside, caught sight of him. They ran indoors crying, "Pa! Pa!"

John Cranston came out, followed by the rest of the children, who all lined up once again in a row, as if it was a trick they liked to perform.

Cranston looked hollow-eyed and stood silent when Gus reached him. Rarely had Gus seen anyone more miserable.

"I've brought your wife's coffin, Mr. Cranston," Gus told him, which had to be one of the most obvious things ever said.

One of the young girls cried, "Oh, look, Papa! It's so pretty."

They broke ranks then, and all gathered round to

peer into the cart. Their eyes went wide.

"Well, now," Gus said, "I was going to attempt some carving, as I said, but I'm more of a rough-and-ready carpenter, and no great hand with that."

John Cranston raised reddened eyes to him. "You did this?"

"No, Mr. Cranston. I'm no artist, either. A—an acquaintance helped me out."

Cranston extended one work-roughened hand and touched a painted flower. "Them's pretty." He echoed his daughter. "Betsy ain't never had anything so pretty as this in her whole life. That's a heart."

"To lie above her head," Gus confirmed.

The children all touched the lid, except the youngest, who was too short to reach.

"That's for Mama?"

John Cranston began to weep. "Thank you, Mr. Wright. You don't know what this means to me."

Not used to seeing a grown man cry, Gus cleared his throat. "Would you like me to take it inside and help settle Mrs. Cranston in?"

"I would most assuredly appreciate that."

The interior of the little house seemed barren in the extreme. Mrs. Cranston lay in her bed, there being nowhere else to put her. Cranston and the oldest daughter, Rebecca, had washed the body and dressed her in what must be her best dress, a dingy brown garment.

Gus placed the coffin in the center of the room, there being but the one room and a loft. He leaned the decorated coffin lid—easily the brightest thing in the place—up against it.

"Neighbors will come," Mr. Cranston said

brokenly. "My neighbor, Jed Elliot, says he'll bring his horse and wagon, for takin' her to the burying ground."

Gus nodded and turned for the door. Cranston seized his arm. "Thank you, Mr. Wright. I'll see you paid—somehow—and soon as I can. And I'll pay a bit extra for that decoration."

"Don't worry about paying extra, Mr. Cranston. And whenever you can pay, that will be fine."

Cranston looked back at the coffin. "Right fittin', that is. When she goes in the ground, she'll be takin' my heart."

Love was a funny thing, Gus reflected as he trundled the empty cart home. It made a man and a woman—two ordinary people—decide to marry and rely upon one another. It had presumably caused John Cranston to bring his wife out here, hoping for a better life, where she'd ended up with nothing except a painted wreath of flowers on her coffin. The best the man could give her.

Yet no one could deny John Cranston loved his wife, as much as Curtis Randolph did. Maybe more.

Gus shook himself. Nobody ever promised life would be easy. It was one of the things his ma taught him after his father died, leaving them with nothing.

"This life is a struggle, Angus, from the cradle to the grave. The measure of a man, or a lad, is found in how he faces adversity, with honesty and with his dignity intact."

Gus had done his best, he sincerely had, to live by that rule. While surviving beneath Silas Groat's iron fist, he'd clung to the fact that his dignity was the one thing Groat couldn't take. Though there had been times he'd been convinced he might lose even that.

One thing he knew for certain—he'd better not ever fall in love. For, as witnessed in the eyes of John Cranston, there lay the greatest vulnerability of all.

Chapter Seven

Phoebe, watching from the shadowed doorway, saw the tall, lanky figure appear like something out of a mad dream. He pushed the cart across the railroad tracks and came on steadily, kicking up little clouds of dust.

He might have been laughable, this undertaker with his fantastical top hat and his elbows sticking out at angles, but Phoebe felt no desire to laugh. Because this man cared about people—enough to try and give a poor woman a lovely resting place.

A rare thing, such caring. She'd learned that much, had met far too many people whose motives ranged from greed to the lust for power, to sheer cruelty for cruelty's sake. Oh, her mother loved her dearly, sure, and Emil had proved good to her. But Emil's motives, so she believed, rested upon lust.

As did those of so many men. Her eyes narrowed as she watched Angus Wright enter the yard in front of his shop. She would have to be careful not to seduce him right out of his gentlemanliness.

For seduce him she might need to do, if Emil didn't turn up.

And maybe—just maybe because he had those lovely, kindly eyes.

The thought shocked her so much, she stiffened where she stood.

Gus settled the cart alongside the building and came in. His gaze sought and found her in the gloom.

"Everything all right here? Has Ned come back yet?"

"Yes, everything is quiet, and no, nobody came."

"I just stopped to leave off the cart before going to get us some supper."

"Sit down first, and catch your breath. There's no hurry." Phoebe went in back and fetched him a mug of water. When she returned, he still stood with his hat in his hands.

What nice hair he had. A shame he kept it covered so much of the time.

"Sit," she told him again, and handed him the cup. "Tell me, did they like the painted coffin?"

He lowered himself into a chair. "Did they! Couldn't believe it. Mr. Cranston, he wept."

Phoebe clapped her hands. "Oh, I am pleased. And did he pay you?"

"Not yet. I doubt he has the money, and in fact I'm not sure he ever will." He gave her a rueful look. "I suppose you think I'm a pretty poor businessman, giving my wares away for free—especially since you put work in on this one."

"No, I do not think you a fool." Phoebe perched on a second chair. *I think you're a good man.* She didn't say that aloud. "Charity can be good for the soul."

"About your situation—" he began.

She didn't let him finish. "I was thinking while you were gone, perhaps other people in town—customers— would appreciate a decorated coffin. You could charge more. That way, I'd be earning my keep."

"That's what—"

"Why don't you bring in another coffin lid? You have nearly half a dozen out there."

"Never know when death will make a run."

His sonorous tone made her want to laugh. She didn't. "I'll paint one up, and we'll put it out there on display. It will make a good advertisement."

Gus Wright sighed. "When were ye thinking of doing that?"

"This afternoon. We have the paint. I can go without supper. Let me get to work while the light's still good."

"You said before how hungry you were. All you've had is that biscuit. Anyway, after that long push, I'm starving."

"Then bring in the lid before you go fetch the food." She reached out and touched his hand. "Let me pay my way."

He rose and clapped the hat back on his head. "All right. But where do ye plan to sleep tonight?"

"I thought perhaps here, in the corner of the shop."

"This is where Ned sleeps."

"Then you'll need to have a talk with Ned, won't you. Explain things."

His eyebrows soared. "Explain things?"

"Well—not things as they truly are, but things as you want him to believe they are. For the time being."

He glanced out the door. "If this Emil went to Laramie, how soon do you think he'll backtrack and find you here?"

Phoebe experienced a pang. Did he want so badly to get rid of her, this kindly yet somber man who was at once so graceful and so awkward? She didn't know why that should hurt, but it did.

"It depends on how long it takes him to figure out what's happened to me. Is there any transportation, other than the train?"

"He could hire a horse. Or there's the stage."

"A few days, then. Please, Mr. Wright, let me stay till he comes."

She put what appeal she could in her eyes. When his gaze returned to her face, she saw him waver.

"Well," he said at last, "there's nowhere for you to go tonight. But when Ned comes back, you let me do the explaining, all right?"

"Whatever you say."

He stuffed a hand into his pocket, jingled some coins, and went out.

Not till he'd gone did Phoebe realize he'd forgotten to bring in a coffin lid. Making sure her braid was well tucked up inside Ned's ratty cap, she stepped out into the bright sunlight and dragged in the nearest one. It was heavier than she expected, and she concluded Gus Wright must be stronger than he looked, if he hoisted not only the lids but the coffins with apparent ease.

She was already deeply engrossed with her design when he returned. The scent of food caught her nose, and her stomach rumbled a response.

She leaped up from her crouch in front of the coffin lid.

"How did that get in here?" Wright asked. He held a little pail in his hand and, when Phoebe turned, she caught him eyeing her posterior.

"I brought it in."

"Ye went outside?" His voice rose in a rusty protest. "Did anybody see ye?"

"I don't think so. Goodness, what's in the pail? It

47

smells wonderful."

"Stew."

"Come in back. Let's eat."

He glanced at the coffin lid on the way, and as they entered the back room he said, "That's different from the other one."

"Yes. Not everybody's going to want a heart. I could paint a plain wreath, as it's common practice to lay a wreath on a grave. For this one, I decided on a posey of flowers. Roses, since I have red, and forget-me-nots."

He set the pail on the table.

"Where do you keep your plates?" she asked, nearly salivating.

In answer, he stepped to a cupboard and handed down two plates from on high. They were made of tin.

Phoebe had heard of tin plates; she'd never before seen any. At home, she'd dined off fine china. Now, though, she felt hungry enough to eat from a trough.

She set the plates on the rough planks of the table and eyed the pail eagerly.

Manners, Phoebe. She heard Mother's voice in her mind. She would need to eat slowly and with decorum—like a lady—despite her desire to wolf the food down.

"Go ahead," Wright told her. "Dish up."

She filled both plates, using a ladle he handed her. The aroma nearly overwhelmed her.

From his pocket he produced several biscuits—not the frosted variety he'd given her earlier but plain baking powder ones, all wrapped in a napkin.

They ate. Phoebe did her best to restrain herself, but the stew went down quickly, and she chased the last of the gravy around with her biscuit.

She caught Gus Wright staring at her then.

"My word, that was good."

He peered into the pail. "Finish what's there."

"Oh, I couldn't." His portion was only half gone.

Calmly, he scraped out the contents of the pail onto her plate.

Suddenly, Phoebe's throat closed and tears filled her eyes. Kindness. "You are being very good to me."

He looked alarmed. "Here, now. No need to get fashed."

Phoebe gazed into his mild, blue eyes, and something unexpected happened to her heart—a softening. Or perhaps it was longing.

Oh, to live always in the warmth of such kindness.

"I'm not upset." She wiped at her eyes. "I'm merely—" But she had no words for what she felt.

"Tired and famished?" he suggested, understanding now filling his face. "You know, ye were in a dead faint when I opened up that casket."

"There wasn't much air inside. As I've said, when it got warm, there were times I feared I would suffocate."

"Aye, that is a well-constructed casket. And it was a mad idea, letting yourself be hammered inside, if ye do not mind me saying so."

Phoebe didn't mind. "I hated the sound of those nails going in, and I was desperate for water."

"Plenty o' water here. We share a well with other businesses here about. But you'd best let me fetch from it, at least till folks get used to the idea of another lad round the place."

"All right," Phoebe agreed, with uncharacteristic

meekness. With her belly full, and Gus Wright sitting across the table from her, she felt less of a desire to fight.

"Ned will be back soon."

"What shall we tell him?"

Gus crumbled his biscuit. "I've been pondering that. I hate lying to the lad. He's all too ready to tell a falsehood on his own, and since he's been with me, I've been doing my best to persuade that out o' him."

"How did he happen to come to you?"

"He was sent from the East with some other lads— orphans, like him—to work on local farms. The farmer he went to was a right bastard—pardon my language. Fortunately for Ned, the fellow died."

"Oh!"

"Ned came to me, to order the coffin, sent by the man's widow. I took one look at him and could see his misery."

Yes, he would. He must see a lot with those eyes— her hunger, Ned's pain.

"He still had time to serve on his contract with the farmer. I traded the widow a coffin for him."

"You bought him—with a coffin?"

"I didn't say that. Ned's free. When he gets a little older, he wants to head farther west, to California."

Phoebe gave him a discerning look. "Is that what you do? Take in strays? Ned—now me. I'm surprised you don't have a mangy dog."

A rare and beautiful smile burst across his face, like sunlight breaking through rain. "I do. Her name's Selkie, and she should be coming around for her feed any time now." He indicated the broken biscuit, which he'd mixed with the remnants of his stew. "Here's her supper."

Phoebe laughed, and Gus joined in, a deep, rich chuckle as unexpected as the smile. She longed to reach across the table and touch his hand, to move closer to this man. Instead, she asked, "What will you tell Ned?"

"As I say, I hate to lie. But for now, I think I'll tell him you're a relative, who came in on the train. A cousin, perhaps."

"Cousin?"

"Aye. The son of an uncle who came to America after—after I came west."

"Name?"

"Eh?"

"Name of your uncle. Let's call him Jesse. Jesse Wright."

"All right. It doesn't much matter."

"It does, if we're to keep the story straight." Phoebe widened her eyes at him. "I find it helps, thinking of it as a story rather than a lie."

He studied her face. "That's what you do, is it? And is this all a story you're telling me now, Miss Corbet?"

"No. It's the truth."

A plaintive whine came from out back. Gus got to his feet, the tin plate in his hand. He paused long enough to say, "I suppose it makes no difference."

"Why?"

"You won't be here all that long, will you?"

He stepped out to feed the hopeful dog. Phoebe remained at the table, a sudden ache in her heart.

Chapter Eight

Phoebe came awake from a nightmare of terrible proportions, to find someone staring at her. With a gulp, she gazed back while reality reassembled itself in her mind.

Ned. Her fevered brain supplied the name. She'd met him last night when he came home. They'd bedded down in separate corners of the workshop, with a number of coffins between them.

She certainly hadn't expected to become an object of his attention.

He had huge, dark eyes, now filled with curiosity. He sat cross-legged on the floor beside her. How long had he been there?

"You all right?" he asked.

Phoebe nodded and pushed herself up from her blanket—her sole possession in the world, other than the clothing she wore. And even the blanket had been given to her by Gus Wright.

She hoped Ned hadn't studied her too closely and noted—well, her bosom. Fortunately for her, it was a small bosom, small enough that the blue shirt she wore covered it. At least, she hoped so.

Would Ned ask why she slept in her cap?

He must have come from his bed across the way, and his head lay bare. He had wild, black hair, and his shirt was unbuttoned.

"Did you have a bad dream?" he inquired. "You were thrashing around and mumbling. Did you dream someone was beating you? That happens to me sometimes. I dream the farmer I used to work for, Mr. Matthews, is on me again. He used to beat me if I didn't work fast enough."

Phoebe blinked at him. He hadn't talked so much last night. Of course, it had been later than expected when he arrived home. Gus had spoken to him about it.

In a kindly manner, of course.

Gus.

The thought of him sent a kind of jolt from Phoebe's brain downward. She wanted to see him, sooner rather than later.

She shoved herself up higher and looked at the closed door that led to his quarters. She wondered how he'd look while asleep.

"I—I'm all right," she told Ned. "I did have a bad dream, though."

He continued studying her. "Mean masters are the worst, aren't they? A trial, and no mistake. Except for Gus. Gus has been real good to me. He's sending me to school when it starts in a few days. Maybe you can come along with me."

"Uh—" Phoebe's brain, usually quite nimble, didn't seem to be operating with its usual velocity.

A distraction kept her from answering. A small, scruffy dog crept out from behind Ned and edged its way onto his lap.

"This must be Selkie." Phoebe held out a hand. The dog shrank into the crook of Ned's elbow. She glanced questioningly at the boy.

"She's afraid of people," he said simply. "Gus says

53

somebody must have been awful cruel to her."

Phoebe couldn't imagine why anyone would be cruel to such an animal. Selkie couldn't weigh above twenty pounds and looked like nothing more than a ball of raggedy gray fur. Not a vicious bone in her body.

"She must have had a litter, some place," Ned elaborated. "Gus went looking for them when Selkie showed up at the back door, but he never found 'em."

Phoebe pictured the tall undertaker swamped by a litter of pups—it wasn't hard to do. "So he kept her?"

"He said he wouldn't, but whenever she turned up for food, he fed her." Ned grinned. "He's the one who named her, too. He says a selkie is some kind of magical critter, in Scotland."

So Angus Wright was fanciful as well as kind. "How did she get in here?"

"I let her in the shop after Gus goes to bed, and she sleeps with me. It's a comfort, and keeps the nightmares away. Don't tell."

Phoebe shook her head. The lies were piling up. No, stories—they were *stories.*

"So," Ned settled more comfortably, "what do you want to be, once you're grown?"

Phoebe thought about it. "An artist."

"Yeah—I saw that coffin lid you're painting. How'd you learn to do that?"

"My—old master."

"It's real good. But a little bit sissy, ain't it? Being an artist, I mean."

Phoebe momentarily stopped breathing. "Lots of great artists are men."

"Oh, yeah?"

"Michelangelo, Rembrandt—"

54

Ned made a face. "Never heard of 'em. Maybe we'll learn about 'em in school. Don't know, though, since Gus says I'll probably just learn to cypher and read. I've already picked up a few things, you know? I'm not too bad at cyphering, but reading's hard."

"So what are you planning to be?"

"I'm saving up to get me a gun." Again, Ned's face brightened. "I'd like to be a hired gun some day, like Mr. Standish used to be. You know Mr. Standish?"

Phoebe shook her head.

"He helps run the livery now. He gave up the life." Ned clearly didn't approve. "For love, so Gus says."

"Mercy!"

"Dumb, right? I mean, who'd give up a gun for a woman?"

"I can't imagine."

"Neither can I. I'm planning to train up, then go travel, and be the best in the West."

A remarkable—if ill-fated—ambition.

"Are there a lot of outlaws in town?"

"Gus says Wylder's where gunslingers come to die. Of course, it's good for business."

"You don't want to follow Gus and become an undertaker, then?"

Ned shuddered. "I don't like touchin' 'em, though I help if Gus asks." Ned eyed her again. "Hey, if you stay, maybe you can be his 'prentice."

"I don't think I'll be staying that long." Phoebe got to her feet. "If you'll excuse me, I need the outhouse."

"Me too. Want to have a pissing contest?"

"Uh—I don't think so." Leaving the boy and dog, which now slept in his lap, Phoebe fled.

****

Gus leaned against the doorway of the shop, careful not to block too much light, and watched Phoebe work. It had taken her most of the morning, but she'd almost finished the design on the second coffin lid, working carefully and with precision.

It nearly took his breath away. She'd painted a spray of flowers, roses and forget-me-nots like she said, the stems all tied with a bow that looked so real he wanted to touch it. The very colors brightened the dim room.

He just couldn't stop watching. Or maybe it was the woman from whom he couldn't bear to remove his eyes.

She was so beautiful, quite possibly the loveliest thing he'd ever seen. Even with her hair tucked up under the raggedy cap, and dressed in boy's clothing. Maybe because she'd dressed in boy's clothing. The view from the rear, when she moved along the propped coffin lid, well, yes, that also took his breath away.

Her concentration, though, appeared total. And the delicate way she moved her hands fascinated him. Her smile, when at last she turned and caught him watching, gave him a thrill.

"There. I believe it is done. Let it dry very well before you put it outside."

Gus, lacking proper words, said nothing.

She rose and came to stand beside him, giving the project a judicious look. In truth, she wasn't much taller than Ned and barely topped Gus's shoulder. "Don't you like it?"

"I do, Miss Phoebe."

"Better call me Phil." Even though Ned had been sent off to run an errand. "Just to get in the habit." She stared him right in the eye. "Not that I'll be here all that long."

He nodded, a sick, sinking feeling weighting his gut.

"How much will you charge for a decorated coffin?"

Gus took off his hat and shoved his fingers through his hair. "Don't rightly know. I charge just a dollar for a plain one. Problem is, most folks can't afford that. Maybe a dollar-ten?"

"I think you can ask more."

He lifted an eyebrow. "You are going to want your cut."

"No." She propped her hands on her hips. "I'm doing this in an effort to pay you back for helping me. When did you say the next train comes?"

"Two days."

"My cargo may well be on it. Then I can pay you back properly."

"I don't want any repayment."

"You deserve it. Besides, Ned says you want to add on to this place."

Gus glanced around. "I'd like a better showroom. And bigger quarters, so Ned could sleep in back and I'd have a room of my own."

One, maybe, to share with a woman. A mad idea, and one he usually dismissed as quick as he could. What woman would want to be touched by hands that touched corpses? Besides, he didn't want just any woman.

Damn it all, what was wrong with him?

"I've been thinking, this decorated lid will be your best advertisement. But I should do up another one—

less flowery, maybe. Something a man would like. What other colors of paint can you get?"

"Not much. I could ask Mr. Wylder, at the mercantile, to order in. but—"

"I won't be here that long?"

Gus flushed. "I'm just trying to be practical. You won't, will you?"

She gnawed on her lip. "I can get a number of lids painted up fairly quickly, if you can build more coffins."

"I can. Think I could knock 'em up in my sleep."

"Bring in another lid from outside. I'll come up with something."

"Would it help if I sanded the lids off better?"

"A smooth surface is always best for painting designs."

"Let me do that first." Gus experienced a rare flash of enthusiasm. "Then I'll go down to the mercantile, see what colors I can scare up."

"I can blend colors. Get whatever you can."

"I will."

She reached out to touch his hand, and he felt the effects all the way up to his head.

"We make a good team, Angus Wright."

So they did. But for how long?

Chapter Nine

Gus peered down the railway line, and his gaze caught a puff of smoke, telling him the train approached. Only a handful of folks waited on the platform in the hot morning sun.

He shifted his feet and felt the sweat trickle down under the brim of his hat. He ran Miss Phoebe's instructions through his mind once again.

Look for a middle-aged fellow in a gray suit. He's not tall, not nearly so tall as you, and has a round head like a boulder, covered with straw-colored hair. If he disembarks, be sure and grab him.

How am I supposed to do that, Miss Phoebe?

Just tell him you're a friend of Miss Corbet, and bring him back here with you.

If he won't come?

He will.

If he's not there—

Then you have to pick up the cargo. It will be tagged for Emil Herzog. Say you're claiming it on his behalf.

What if they refuse to let me have it?

They will, if you use his name.

What kind of package is it?

Plain, brown paper. Maybe the size of two thick books wrapped together.

As he waited, the train appeared and pulled into the

station, snorting steam like some fairy-tale dragon. He condemned himself as ill-suited for this venture. He didn't lie, as a matter of principle, and so had little practice at it. He didn't like the idea of accosting this Emil Herzog, a stranger, but Miss Phoebe was counting on him.

He would carry it through.

Only three passengers disembarked from the train—fewer than usual. Two were women, a mother and daughter, from the ·look of them. A man was waiting on the platform for them, and escorted them away.

The other passenger, male, was tall and elderly. Didn't match Emil Herzog's description.

"Damn," Gus muttered. When the conductor came by, Gus grabbed him. "Any other passengers, sir?"

"Nobody for Wylder. Everyone else is goin' through." The conductor shot him a look. "You expecting somebody?"

"A man by name of Herzog. About your height, wearing a gray suit."

The conductor shook his head. "Sorry, must be the wrong train."

"Possibly his plans changed. He said if he couldn't make it, I should collect a package for him. It's important."

Another sharp look. "You sure about that?"

"I am." Gus made a show of searching his pockets. "I have a letter—"

"What was that name again?"

"Herzog. Emil Herzog."

"Come on into the baggage car. You're in luck, not much baggage this trip, either. Not even the mail. I don't have time to look through it, but you're welcome."

"Thank you," Gus said, and meant it.

The conductor shrugged. "You look like an honest man."

Gus cringed as he leaped up into the car. Packages and parcels—about twenty of them—were scattered in piles, and trying not to feel furtive, he began with those closest to hand. A careful man, he made a methodical search, looking first for a package matching Phoebe's description. Only one or two fit. One was addressed to a woman in Buford. The other to an army officer at Fort Laramie.

He then set about a closer search, checking addresses on every bundle. The interior of the car felt like an oven, even with the door open. When he'd turned over each package twice, he straightened, fighting for breath.

It felt good to jump down onto the sunny platform. What now?

Miss Phoebe would be disappointed.

The conductor called from farther down the track, "You find it?"

"Not there."

"Must have missed the train, just like your friend."

"Thanks for your time."

The man gave him a wave and moved off. Gus loped away home, making the most of his long stride.

Phoebe stood watching from the doorway of the shop. Her gaze pounced on him. "Where is it?"

"Not there." He pushed her back into the shop with a hand on her shoulder. Any excuse, these past three days, to touch her—even though he knew he shouldn't.

She stared. "Emil?"

"Not on the train."

"Are you sure? Maybe I should go—"

"No, Miss Phoebe. There were only a few passengers. Herzog wasn't among them."

"Drat! I'm getting worried now. What could have happened to him?"

Gus shook his head, removed his hat, and shrugged out of his coat. "I have no idea."

"But," she gazed at him with pleading, blue eyes, "the package—it must have been there. Mother was to send it on the next train."

Gus shook his head again. "Let me ask you, why didn't you and this Emil fellow just take the package right along with you? Why send it after?"

"We thought if we were apprehended it would be safer not to have the stolen goods on us. It must have been there. You could have missed it—"

"No, Miss Phoebe. I searched that whole car. Nothing addressed to Emil Herzog, or matching the description you gave me."

"Perhaps—"

"I examined them all."

She sagged where she stood. "Mother may have been prevented from sending it. What am I to do?"

Reluctantly, Gus suggested, "Go on to Laramie." He liked having her here, maybe a bit too much.

"But…" She began to pace, distractedly. "If Emil were there, surely he'd have made his way back here by now. It's been three days. And he left me nailed inside a casket." She turned to Gus, looking rueful. "I know it must be difficult to believe, looking at me now, but Emil—well, he truly does have rather a *tendre* for me."

"*Tendre*?"

"He's sweet on me."

It wasn't difficult to believe. Even dressed as a lad, with her shining black hair all hidden and her slim curves well covered, she shone. Gus might have a bit of a *tendre* for her himself.

Passionately, she declared, "I don't think he'd abandon me."

"I see."

"Therefore, logically, something must have happened to him. And to the jewels also. Oh!" She raised her hands to her face. "What have I done?"

"Why don't you sit down and tell me the whole of it, from the beginning?"

"I'm not sure that's a good idea."

Gus stiffened. For the last three days, he'd been hiding her, feeding her, and lying to Ned for her. Fortunately, Ned had decided to stay with his friend Andy Arkwright for a few days before school started.

Did Phoebe imply, now, she didn't trust him? That hurt.

Since he was basically an honest man, he asked, "Don't ye trust me, Miss Corbet?"

That made her turn her gaze on him. "Oh, yes. It's not that. I just hate dragging you any deeper into my troubles. If you knew it all," she gnawed on her lip, "I'm afraid you might wind up where Emil is—wherever that is."

A customer appeared at the door, asking about the decorated coffin lid on display out front. Gus donned his hat and coat and went out, while Phoebe melted into the back room.

The fellow just wanted to ask the price of the

coffin, and talk about the decoration. Passersby had been doing that for days.

Gus had carefully sanded down two more lids. Phoebe had one nearly ready for display.

When the man took himself off, Gus returned inside. He found Phoebe sitting at the table in the back room with her head in her hands.

He sat down opposite her.

"I don't know what to do." She raised her eyes and looked at him. "If I don't recover the jewels, I won't be able to pay you what I owe."

"Don't worry about that."

"But I p-promised. And I always do keep my promises."

A thief who always kept her promises?

She folded her hands on the table. Despair filled her eyes. "I knew it was a mad plan, from the first. But I was just so angry at my stepfather. I wanted to strike back at him, and like I said before, to get my just due."

"Revenge, rather than justice?"

Phoebe studied him for an instant. "Maybe. But it's all come apart."

Gus covered her hands with one of his. She didn't jerk away. "So tell me."

"It's a long story—"

"We have plenty of time."

Chapter Ten

Gus Wright, so Phoebe decided, had the most seductive eyes she'd ever seen. The way he looked at her made her want to confide in him and assured her that her secrets would be safe—that she'd be safe with him.

But who would keep him safe, in turn? He might well seduce her with his kindness, but she didn't want him to pay a hefty price.

As Emil had, perhaps. And her mother—what had happened to Mother?

"My parents emigrated to America from France when I was very small. Father was a jeweler, back in Rouen—a good one. Mother served as his assistant. He brought his skills, and a lot of stock, to the new world. We lived in New York for a time, but I don't remember that. Father wanted to keep moving west." She gave a bleak smile. "He liked being a big fish in a small pond."

Gus nodded.

"He built a thriving business in Cedar Rapids—that's in Iowa. But he got sick, and worsened over a long period of time. Mother and I carried on, under his supervision. He said, always, I had a talent for design."

"You're a fine artist, and no mistake," Gus said encouragingly.

"Father's jewelry designs were in demand all the way back East. By the time I was thirteen, he was producing my designs also. When something sold, he always put away a percentage for me, in a special account. My security for the future, he called it." She paused. "He died when I was fifteen."

Here, Phoebe's voice failed her. The long-debilitating illness had caught up with Leonard Corbet and taken much from all of them in its progression.

She remembered holding his hand, much as Gus now held hers, as he died, how he'd looked at her and said, "My beautiful daughter." His only child. "So much talent. Promise me you'll use that talent to light up your life."

Far more than Phoebe's father had passed, that day. Her security, her happiness, and much of her innocence had also gone, though she didn't know it then. Her father left a devastated wife and daughter behind, along with a thriving business and a fortune in jewels.

In her extreme grief, Phoebe's mother struggled to run that business, and though Phoebe believed she would one day be able to take over, at fifteen she was still too young.

When Father's associate and fellow jeweler, Jasper Dent, stepped in, Phoebe's mother agreed to let him help run the business. They'd married a year later, when Phoebe was sixteen.

She learned a lot, and swiftly, then. Dent, who'd always made Phoebe uncomfortable, soon proved what kind of man he was—a martinet who laid down the law and expected his new wife and stepdaughter to toe the line. He'd immediately taken over all operations of the business and, though he treated Phoebe's mother well enough—at least in public—he didn't bother to pretend he cared for Phoebe.

That didn't keep him from exploiting her designs, putting them into production and taking full credit for them.

In time she figured out he was, in essence, stealing from her.

"I'm ashamed to say how long it took me," she admitted to Gus now, telling the tale. "But continuing with my designs brought me a measure of comfort. And he claimed he'd put the money from sales of my designs away for me, as Father always did."

"He didn't?"

Phoebe shook her head. "I found out when I wanted to withdraw some funds, to reinvest in what I thought of as my branch of the business. I went to the bank and discovered the account Father had set up for me no longer existed.

"When I charged Jasper with it, he laughed at me. Laughed! Of course, Mother got dragged into it. He told us the business now belonged to him—all of it. There was nothing we could do.

"I think their marriage—such as it was—broke then. My mother is a very loyal woman. But she never loved Jasper. She missed my father terribly, and ached for him every day.

"She and I hatched a plan, and spoke of it only in French, so Jasper would not understand. Emil was one of Father's customers and a friend—as I say, and he'd developed feelings for me. I wanted to steal back from Jasper what was rightfully mine. We couldn't have made it work without Emil."

"What did you intend to do, after you made good your escape?"

Phoebe grimaced ruefully. "Emil said we could set

up shop elsewhere, after lying low for a time, that is. Now that I think on it, I suppose he imagined him and me being together."

She'd been a fool about that, too. She should have known Emil would not take such a risk without the promise of reward.

Everyone wanted something.

Except, perhaps, this man sitting opposite her.

Upon that thought, little Selkie trotted into the room through the open shop door. Slinking past Phoebe's side of the table, she took up a post at Gus's knee.

He patted her with his free hand.

"I don't believe Emil would betray me."

"It seems not."

"I'm afraid Jasper discovered our scheme somehow and came after us. Or sent someone. When the jewels first disappeared—and I assure you, I took only what was left of my own designs—we pretended it had been an outside job."

"And he believed this?"

"He did. Or he pretended to. Jasper's a devious and twisted man. What if he had us followed? What if Emil's dead?"

"Then Jasper will be looking for ye. Unless he's recovered the jewels."

Miserably, she said, "And even if he has, he's not the man to let what we did go unpunished. And my mother is still in his hands."

Gus suggested, "Maybe you should go home."

"I'll be arrested if I do. I was already accused of the theft, you know. Jasper threatened to put me in prison. It was Emil who hatched the plan to get me away in the casket, which was made where he worked."

"Ah, perhaps if this Jasper has recovered the jewels and you fess up, he will agree not to pursue your arrest. And you can make sure your ma is all right."

She raised her eyes to his face. "If you wish to be rid of me—"

"It's not that." Gus's throat worked. "That's the last thing I want."

They gazed at one another. Phoebe's heart fluttered in her breast.

Back in Cedar Rapids, she'd been paid compliments by the foremost flowers of society. Courted by the most eloquent of men. She'd enjoyed the attentions of some, and spurned most.

Sitting here now, she tried to discern what such individuals—the upper crust, so to speak—would think of this man with his eccentric clothing and bony elbows.

They would look down on him was what. They'd sneer at his appearance and lack of means.

In truth, they weren't fit to carry his shoes. And his steady regard raised the tempo of her pulse the way no pretty words or slick manners ever had, back home.

That thought made her say softly, "You should send me away. I've complicated your life most terribly."

"You haven't."

"I have. You've had to lie about me to Ned and your customers. And now it looks like I won't be able to repay you the way I promised."

"I never cared about the money." Well, that seemed fairly obvious, given the way he lived—and his kind, generous heart. "But, Miss Phoebe, I do want to see you safe."

Sudden tears stung Phoebe's eyes.

He went on, "If Emil has disappeared and your plan's fallen apart, if you're worried about your ma, I think you need to go home."

"Perhaps you are right." She couldn't expect to play the part of a boy forever. Someone would tumble to the truth, eventually.

Worse, what if Jasper sent someone after her? What if that someone had already seized or punished Emil? Gus Wright could be next. He might pay a terrible price for helping her.

That thought had her stumbling to her feet. Gus, still holding her hands, arose also, and the dog shied away with a whine of protest. They stood, separated only by the table.

"I must return at once to Cedar Rapids."

An emotion flooded his eyes. Was that regret? He nodded.

"But how?" she asked. "I have no way to buy a ticket home. No hope of any."

"And if someone is looking for ye, they'll keep watch on the trains, so I would expect."

"Yes."

"I can perhaps find other clothing for ye."

"Oh? Women's clothes?"

"No. The ladies at the church gave us some things for Ned. A number of the garments are too big for him." Gus's gaze measured her. "Should fit ye, though."

"So I'd have to travel on the train as a boy?"

"If Jasper has sent men after ye, if he does not come himself, you just may pass. If he sees ye with his own eyes—" Gus shook his head.

"I don't look enough like a boy?"

"I'm amazed ye've passed this long."

"Not many here in Wylder have seen me." Just a few customers in passing, and from the back they might have thought she was Ned.

"Perhaps," Gus suggested, "you should send your mother a letter. Does her husband intercept her mail?"

"Not usually. It's a good idea. I can write in French, so he cannot read it, even if it's intercepted. But Mr. Wright, that will take days. For a letter to get to Cedar Rapids and another to get back to me? Days and days."

"So?" His fingers tightened on hers. "You're welcome to stay, meanwhile."

"Am I?" Stay, and endanger him? "Is that wise?"

His lips tightened. "My old master, he to whom I used to be apprenticed, called me a fool. It was his favorite name to throw at me, amid a host of others. Maybe he was right. But I—I canna see any harm come to ye, if I have a way to prevent it."

The tears filling Phoebe's eyes threatened to overflow.

Gus misread the cause of them. "Here, Miss Phoebe, take heart. Write your letter. Anything might happen in the next few days. Emil may turn up, or the jewels."

"You're a good man, Gus Wright."

His eyes widened. "Me? No."

She stumbled around the table and into his arms.

For days, the desire to touch him had burgeoned in her mind. She'd longed to embrace him, take refuge in him, the way a ship slipped into port.

Now she felt him stiffen with surprise as her body encountered his. A thousand sensations flooded her.

He felt hard and strong, and safe. So tall was he, her head only reached his shoulder. She was able to tuck her cheek up against it. He smelled like wood shavings and warm sunshine, and the particular scent he always brought into a room.

She closed her eyes for a moment, in bliss.

"Miss Phoebe—"

"Hush. Hold me, please. Just for a minute."

His arms closed around her. One hand settled at her back. The other cradled her head with such tenderness the tears in her eyes spilled over.

"What if someone walks in and sees us?" His voice came in a bass murmur.

"They won't."

"They might."

And then, someone did. A step sounded in the outer room, and a voice called, "Mr. Undertaker, you in? I want to ask you 'bout these here fancy coffins."

Gus jerked away from Phoebe, gave her one intense look, and leaped away, into the shop.

Phoebe felt his absence like the coming of winter.

Chapter Eleven

Gus Wright scowled at the coffin lid taking shape beneath his hands. He worked in the sunshine outside his shop, knocking the units together at a tremendous rate. Not because there'd been so many deaths recently in Wylder. He figured there'd been an average number. But because he just kept selling coffins.

The decorated ones. Folk couldn't seem to get enough of them.

He'd sold the one Phoebe painted up with the rose bouquet and the next, with the wreath, in record time. He'd sanded up several more lids, and procured her additional paint. No sooner did she finish a new lid than the coffin got snatched up.

God only knew what people were doing with them.

Well, he supposed he could guess—they put them away for later, which seemed a bit gruesome. Cyrus Haddock, over at the gunsmith's shop, had put his on display out front, which Phoebe called a good investment for his business. He supposed she was right, since several customers had stopped by, saying they'd seen that one.

Phoebe.

For the life of him, Gus couldn't stop thinking about her. Even when he was doing other things, she filled his mind. Ever since she'd embraced him, there in the gloom of his back room—and no, he couldn't mistake that for anything but an embrace—he'd longed to touch her again. Quite shocking thoughts possessed his mind, notions that had no place there.

Like holding her that way for an hour or so, and following it with a kiss. Sitting her on his knee. Filling a whole evening—for they usually spent those together after Ned went to sleep—with kisses. Touching parts of her that lay beneath that worn lad's clothing.

He should be ashamed. God knew he should. Long ago, back in Scotland, his ma had taught him to be respectful of women. The thoughts that now crowded his mind did not seem…well, respectful.

But he'd be damned if he could banish them.

Upon that thought, he felt Phoebe looking at him. He seemed able to tell now whenever she focused her attention his way. In the warmth, he'd opened his collar, stripped off his coat, and rolled up his sleeves to work. He knew he was nothing to look at, but something about the expression in her eyes when he caught her stealing glances made him feel otherwise.

He shot a look toward the doorway, and there she stood, just within the shadows. So far, she'd been introduced to no one from outside. When folks asked who painted the coffin lids—for Gus could scarcely take credit—he said he had a young cousin staying with him who did them up.

Folks marveled over that, said they bet Gus would hate to see his cousin go.

Oh, aye.

He and Phoebe had discussed at length how much to charge for the painted coffins. Since the plain ones Gus knocked together sold for just a dollar, Phoebe insisted the decorated ones should be a dollar and a half.

"That's too much," he protested. "Folks won't pay it."

Only, they had.

Just as well. He still hadn't seen a penny from Mr. Cranston for his wife's coffin. And he'd had to pay Finn Wylder up front for some fancy paints he'd ordered at the mercantile. He wondered if Phoebe would still be here when they came in, and pain tore through his chest.

Jesus, was he dying?

He straightened from his task, and Phoebe threw him a smile. No, not dying. A gift like that could surely keep him clinging to life.

The shadow that was Phoebe suddenly disappeared from the doorway, and a woman came strolling up. That nice Mrs. Standish it was, who ran the bakery. She'd married Buck Standish, who co-owned the livery, earlier this summer. And her young brother, who had come from back East, was friends with Ned.

A graceful woman, she too paused to eye Gus, one foot pointed daintily. Dressed in a plain dark skirt and white blouse, she nevertheless looked elegant with her white-blonde hair piled atop her head.

"Ma'am?" Gus mopped his brow. "Might I help you?"

"Good morning, Mr. Wright. I was hoping to view one of your decorated coffins. I did see the one outside the gunsmith's. Have you no more?"

"Ma'am?" Gus stared at her in alarm. "I hope you don't have need of one." He sincerely liked the little family.

A truly dazzling smile broke across her face. "Oh,

no. I had something else in mind." She peered past him. "Is your cousin here, the one who does the painting?"

Well, and folk had been gossiping. "Aye. He's—a bit shy."

"Then I'll tell you what I have in mind, shall I? You know I run the Wylder Side Bakery."

"Sure do. You've been good to my lad, Ned."

"Ned's proved a good pal to Andy, when he needed one, and he's a fine boy. I definitely don't want a coffin out front." Her eyes danced. "Not quite the inviting atmosphere I wish to cultivate. But I painted our shop sign myself, and I'm better at baking than at making signs."

"Oh." Gus tumbled to the idea. "You want a new sign?"

"I'd love one. Something pretty, with flowers like those on the coffins, and maybe a cake and a loaf of bread, all lettered. Does your cousin do lettering?"

Gus mopped his brow again, with his forearm. "I don't rightly know."

"Maybe you can find out. The sign could be made of pine. That's what I have now."

"Yes, ma'am." Gus glanced at the doorway of the shop. "I can surely ask him."

"I wouldn't be able to pay you much. Perhaps fifty cents? But I could sweeten the deal, so to speak, by providing you with some of my baked goods, free of charge. I know how much Ned enjoys my baking."

"Aye. That would be grand."

"And it would be a good advertisement for you. I'd be willing to tell everyone where I got the sign."

Gus's head spun. It sounded like a wonderful way to expand his business…beyond death, so to speak.

If only Phoebe were staying.

"Let me talk it over with my—er—cousin and I'll get back to ye, Mrs. Standish."

She gave him another smile. "You do that." Did she know something she shouldn't? Suspect he lied? Och, he was a terrible liar.

"Good day now, Mr. Wright."

She moved off in the direction of the livery, on the way to visit with her husband, no doubt.

Carefully, Gus laid aside his hammer and went inside, where the cool air of the shadowy interior enfolded him.

Phoebe stood behind the counter, her eyes large.

"Did ye—"

"I heard," she said. She gusted out a breath. "What a wonderful opportunity! That woman has a shop?"

"The Wylder Side Bakery."

"Everyone would see my work. Our work."

Excitedly, she moved around the counter and seized Gus's hands. She often did that, though he couldn't imagine why. His hands were big and bony, and contrasted ludicrously with her dainty ones.

"I confess, I would very much like to do this for her, make a lovely sign to advertise her business. And ours. Should we?" she asked, her eyes shining.

Ours. There was that word again. "Aye." Troubled, Gus gazed into her eyes. "Yet if ye do not stay—"

The light in her face faded. "Oh, yes, you're right." She gulped a breath. "I will have to make up my mind soon about what I should do. Because I cannot continue to impose upon your k-kindness."

Gus's heart again clenched in his chest, an even more alarming pain. Suddenly, without knowing how it happened, he had her in his arms.

"Ye're welcome," he murmured. "Ye're very welcome to stay. If ye wish."

She lifted her head from his shoulder and gazed into his eyes. "I believe I do."

Did Gus move to kiss her then, or did she press closer and kiss him? He never knew. True, she stretched up on her toes, the better to reach his lips, and her hands crept around his neck.

Or maybe he lifted her, after all. The contact of her mouth and his blasted all his senses, chasing rational thought and filling its absence with pure sensation.

Warmth. Sweetness. A kind of vibrating intensity that stole away all the hurt and aches of the past. She somehow fitted so perfectly there in his arms. His heart opened to take her in. His soul cried out in jubilation.

Him. Gus Wright, kissing a woman in his shop. And, this woman above all others. Madness.

Euphoria.

Not shy about participating, Phoebe dug her fingers into the hair that trailed down his neck and parted her lips for him. When he dove inside—an act he suddenly cherished above breathing—she made a sound of wordless approval that utterly enflamed him. Her cap fell off, and he plunged his fingers into her hair. Ah— soft and luxurious, like what he imagined warm silk to be.

Cradling her in one arm, he drew her tighter against him. He wanted—well, he wanted to be inside her, to make her part of him. At this moment, that felt the most natural of outcomes.

"Oh." Abruptly, Phoebe ended the kiss. Reaching up, she trapped his face between her hands. "Oh,

Angus, what are we to do?"

Shaken, Gus gazed into her eyes, seeing his shock and wonder reflected there.

"I fear…" she whispered, "I fear I'm growing attached to you. But it's impossible, isn't it?"

It was, for half a dozen reasons. Never mind that they got along so well, thought the same in many ways, and failed to annoy one another. And quite apart from how good she felt in his arms. His heart was gaffed like a salmon back in the Spey River, where his pa used to take him fishing before he died.

She was quite possibly the best thing that had ever happened to him, and the least appropriate.

"Aye."

Tears flooded her eyes.

"Do no' weep," he beseeched.

She blinked furiously. "You're right. You deserve better than a sniveling sort of woman, considering how good you've been to me. I need to make a decision about what I should do, take the burden from you."

Gus wanted to tell her she wasn't a burden. Only, she was—hiding her here complicated things with Ned and could make Gus himself a target if anyone came after her.

Despite that, he wanted to tell her she should stay. Quite possibly forever.

He couldn't do that, either. The decision had to be hers. Even though parting with her now would feel like ripping his heart out.

She stepped away from him, picked up her cap, and crammed it back on over all that lovely hair. It didn't matter. She still looked beautiful.

She shot him a burning look he couldn't interpret.

"The train comes tomorrow, yes? If either Emil or the package is not on it, I will make a decision then."

Chapter Twelve

Phoebe awoke and lay very still in her bundle of blankets, listening to the quiet of a Wylder dawn.

Since her arrival here she'd learned that, small as the town might be, it had a rhythm, and a clatter. People here worked hard and laughed often.

Except for her grave undertaker, who gave out his smiles like rare gifts.

She closed her eyes and a picture of him swam into her mind. Thick brown hair, soft blue eyes, and an unspoken air of reassurance. But why did she call him that—*her* undertaker? He wasn't, even though she might wish him to be. Despite how good he'd been to her, how kind, and despite the way yesterday's kiss had made her feel, the best thing she could do was let him go and get out of his life.

That thought caused her to stir restlessly, and she opened her eyes, dismissing the vision. From where she lay, she could see the daylight coming in, and the bottoms of several sets of sawhorses, with the rough pine boards of the coffins set upon them.

She'd watched Gus work on those coffins—she liked the way he worked, with calm absorption. When he worked, he stripped off the long frock coat and rolled up his sleeves. She liked his forearms, corded with lean muscle, and his hands, gentle but competent. She wondered—like a wanton—how the rest of his body looked. The question made her shiver where she lay.

Oh, yes, she had feelings for the undertaker. Who would ever have imagined it could be so?

She might be a deceiver and a thief, at least in her stepfather's eyes, but when it came to Gus Wright, she would be honest with herself. Angus Wright, she corrected. She delighted in the burr that colored his voice, and she loved his name.

Angus. Angus Gordon Wright.

There must be a story behind his presence here in Western America—his escape from the wretched Silas Groat—though she hadn't yet got all of it out of him.

She blinked again. Beyond the half-built coffins, as she knew, lay Ned in his nest, not unlike her own. On the far side of the dividing wall, Angus occupied his narrow bed.

Oh, how she wished she were there with him!

That thought shocked her so much she sat up and leaned against the wall. Feeling proprietary about the undertaker would do no good. Jasper must have tumbled to her scheme. Had he sent someone after her? Was poor Emil dead?

And what about Mother? If Jasper knew she, Phoebe, had traveled west, he would suspect Mother knew. Would he retaliate against her? She might pretend she'd known nothing about the theft and escape. That didn't mean he'd believe her.

She rose and Ned came into view, all wrapped up in his blankets with Selkie in his arms. She stretched. The floor made a hard bed, nothing like her eiderdown back home.

How quiet it was, enough to let her hear Ned's soft

breathing. On impulse, she tiptoed to the door of the back room, opened it carefully, and peered in.

Very little light penetrated here, just enough to let her see. The space, not large, was crowded with the iron stove where they cooked, the table and chairs, and Gus's bed.

She caught her breath. He lay on his back, deeply asleep, one cheek turned upward. Covered to the waist with a blanket, he lay with his chest bare, his brown hair tossed into tufts and curls.

He looked like a boy lying there, yet so unlike a boy her heart began to pound.

Hastily, she closed the door. Shutting her eyes tight, she prayed that either Emil or the jewels would be on today's train. Then she could do the undertaker a favor, and get out of his life.

****

It felt like a bad dream, one that had plagued Gus so frequently since first he fled west—overwhelming dread, just as if his old master once more loomed over him. Only this was no dream or memory of ducking Silas Groat's fist.

Instead, he was back on the platform at the train station, kicking his heels and watching for the trail of steam that announced the train's approach. A few other people waited with him. A gentleman with a satchel at his feet, who must be heading farther west. A woman with two small children, a clerk from Wylder's mercantile who loitered even as Gus did, probably expecting a delivery. Gus had nodded to the man and henceforth kept to himself.

No conversationalist, him. And he didn't want anyone overhearing his business.

He thought of Phoebe, anxiously awaiting his return, and he looked at the sky for help. For once, the sun didn't beat down at him like a hammer. In fact, it looked fit to rain.

Hardly a good omen. Only—well, Gus couldn't decide how he wanted things to turn out. Finding Emil would be good for Phoebe, but it would most likely take her away from here, out of his life.

As it should be. Who was he to think he deserved a woman like Phoebe Corbet?

The train gusted in, exhaling great gouts of steam, and Gus braced himself.

As before, the conductor appeared and passengers disembarked. Once again, there were only a few—a small town like Wylder didn't see too many travelers. A short fellow got off and greeted the woman with the children. An older woman disembarked with assistance from the conductor. A tall man stepped down and promptly captured all Gus's attention.

He wore a good-quality beaver hat and an air of authority. Perhaps thirty years old, he fairly oozed competence, and had a pistol strapped to his side.

Definitely not the errant Emil. Phoebe had described Emil Herzog as short, with straw-colored hair. Even from this distance, Gus noted this fellow's hair was brown.

He looked, and smelled, like trouble.

Avoiding him, Gus stepped away toward the baggage car. No one else disembarked, and the tall man stood where he was, sweeping the platform with care. His gaze found Gus, focused for an instant, and dismissed him as unimportant.

It felt a little like being a wee mouse and having

the cat consider you as prey.

"Mr. Undertaker," the conductor greeted him, the same man as last time. "You still lookin' for your package?"

"I am."

"Come aboard."

Once more, the search proved fruitless. By the time Gus finished, the tall fellow had gone and the platform lay deserted.

Rain began to fall as he loped back to the shop, making dark specks in the dust. It added to Gus's sense of foreboding.

Phoebe waited for him just inside the door, anxiety stark in her eyes. When her gaze met his, he merely shook his head, and she turned away with such disappointment it made him catch his breath.

She was anxious to be gone from here, he thought. She couldn't wait to leave him. Despite the smiles and confidences, despite that flaming kiss, she wanted to recover her treasure, and to be on her way.

Of course she did, he flailed himself. What else had he expected? The charm she employed, the way she sometimes looked at him, all that was an effort to persuade him to let her stay till she could work out her dilemma.

He took off his hat and shook the rain from it. "I'm that sorry, Miss Phoebe. No package. No Emil."

"Not your fault."

Carefully, she moved around the saw horses at the center of the room. She'd already begun work on Mrs. Standish's sign, had sketched in the letters and flowers. Now she turned away from it as if it didn't exist.

"Oh, poor Emil. I fear the worst."

As did Gus. In fact, his dread seemed all out of proportion and centered on more than Emil's absence.

He began, "There was a man—"

Her head turned sharply toward him. "Not Emil?"

"Not Emil, no, but there was something about him—"

"What?"

Gus shook his head. "Don't rightly know."

A voice hailed Gus from outside. "Mr. Undertaker?"

Before he could blink, Phoebe disappeared into the back.

A man entered the shop and stated his business. A cowhand, out at one of the ranches, had been killed in a fall from his horse. They needed a coffin as well as Gus's services to come out, hammer the dead man inside, and escort him to the boneyard.

Distracted, Gus agreed to come. The fellow had a buckboard waiting, which would keep Gus from having to hire one.

A good and profitable day's work. Yet he felt uneasy, leaving Phoebe alone.

He told the man, knowing she could hear him through the connecting door, "Just let me close up shop while I'm gone."

Ned would be home soon to keep Phoebe company. He hoped she'd have the sense to stay put till then.

Chapter Thirteen

Phoebe sat at the rough table in Gus's quarters with her chin in her hand, trying to control the wave of rebellious defiance in her heart.

All the fault of her mother, or so her odious stepfather would say. He often ranted at Mother about it.

You have given her ideas far above herself, you and that father of hers, both. Made her think she has a say in matters where she has not. Certainly she may be permitted to dabble with her little designs. That is where it ends.

Her little designs. Jasper made it sound like a mere pastime, an amusement tantamount to embroidery. For Phoebe, though, her art was a passion, and when it came to jewelry, something beyond that.

It had started early when she'd visited her father in his shop, watched the seemingly magical process of him working gold. The glitter and shine of the jewels dazzled her eyes. Not because they represented wealth—no. She hadn't understood that then. But because the colors spoke to her.

When first she'd begun sketching her designs, it had been because of that—because the jewels spoke to her. A ruby might say it wished to be the sole gem set in a filigreed pendant. A line of sapphires might clamor to be set together.

"My daughter has a talent," Father often said with pride. So yes, perhaps Jasper was right. Her parents had given her big ideas, or at least given her permission to unleash those ideas already inside her.

Born there, perhaps.

Did it matter, then, that she was a woman? If the passion came to roost, was mere gender a reason to deny it?

And had it been so wrong for her to take back the pieces she'd created, born of that passion?

To steal them back.

She blinked at a sudden blur of tears born of consternation. It must be wrong, for just look at the trouble in which it had landed her. Her, and others for whom she cared.

Mother, now at Jasper's mercy. Emil who, well, she couldn't bear thinking about what had happened to him. And Angus—

Yes, she might as well admit the truth. She cared for Angus. Who could fail to care for such a man? So gentle, so earnest. Wounded, somehow, though he chose to disguise it.

And look what she'd done—shared her trouble with him, who least needed it.

She had to make a decision, now that neither Emil nor the jewels had turned up. She owed Angus that, if nothing else.

Unquestionably, she should clear out of his life. But—if she did that, she would quite likely never see him again. Could she bear it? Could she bear missing his smile? The shy and yet fervent expression in his eyes when he looked at her. The low, attractive burr in his voice when he became agitated. That outlandish hat of his, the one she suspected betrayed the true nature of the man. Who would expect a quiet, reserved fellow to sport such a hat? What did it say about him?

Whatever it was, it appealed to her enormously.

She never should have kissed him. Make no mistake about it, that was what had happened. He wouldn't have taken advantage of her, being far too much a gentleman. She did, in fact, take terrible advantage of him—of his patience and his good nature.

She ought to travel on to Laramie, where she could institute a search for Emil.

Who was probably dead.

Or she could return home and support her mother, whom she'd abandoned, and face the music.

She had money for neither venture.

Perhaps she should stay here painting signs and coffins till she saved up her fare. Stay with Angus Wright a little longer. The lack of money made a good excuse. And it lifted a terrible weight from her heart.

She'd just wait till Angus got home from—well, from whatever business with death had called him away. Make no decisions till he returned. Meanwhile, the sound of the rain lulled her, and muted the usual clatter of the Wylder afternoon.

She'd resumed work on Mrs. Standish's sign by the time Ned came home from school.

"Where's Gus?" Ned asked, tossing his primer aside.

"Gone off to see about a dead ranch hand. How was school?"

Ned made a face. "It's hard to sit still so long. I'm bad at my letters, though ciphering's fine." He eyed Phoebe closely. "How come you don't have to go with me?"

"Uh—" Phoebe paused with her paint brush above the wooden slats that formed the sign. Gus had done a fine job of fitting and sanding them. He did not give himself enough credit for the things he did well.

"I expect it's 'cause I'm not going to be staying here for good. Just passing through."

Ned's gaze sharpened. "Yeah? How long before you finish passing through?"

Phoebe turned to face him. "You sorry I'm here, Ned?"

"Not so much. It's just odd how you turned up, you know? Supposed to be Gus's cousin. But he never said anything about any relatives, and you don't look or sound like him."

Phoebe shrugged with feigned carelessness.

"And there's something funny about you."

"Funny? You find me humorous?"

"Not that kind of funny." Ned might have trouble with his letters, but obviously possessed accurate perception. "You don't seem—well, like the rest of us."

"Us?"

"Us boys."

Indeed, she wasn't.

Her cheeks flamed. She measured him with a fierce glance. "Sometimes when people are in trouble, they pretend to be what they're not."

Ned contemplated that. "You in trouble?"

"I might be."

"Well, I don't much care, save as how you might bring trouble down on Gus. He's been right good to me. Like family, almost."

"Yes."

"He don't deserve any trouble."

"I agree."

"And I'll protect him if I can."

"It might help keep him out of trouble if you—well, keep quiet about any thoughts you have about me."

"Well, I know that. I ain't stupid."

Indeed, he was not.

"Just so's you know it."

"Believe me, Ned, I'm very much aware."

"Gus is nice. Maybe a little too nice for this world. He lets folk get off without paying for his coffins, and he sometimes lets people take advantage of him."

What a mature thing to say.

"Now," Ned went on, "if you want to stay here a while painting up some coffins for him, I'll play along. But if I think you're taking advantage of him, I just might have to do something about that."

Phoebe gazed full into Ned's dark eyes. "Like what?"

Ned shrugged his narrow shoulders. "Maybe turn you in to whoever's looking for you."

Phoebe's gaze quickened. "Is someone looking for me?"

"Not yet. I reckon it's a matter of time."

"I respect your position, Ned."

"Yeah, just so's it's understood. I'm gonna go run with Andy Arkwright and some of my other friends. Tell Gus, when he gets home."

"Don't you have school work to do?"

Ned tipped his head at her. "Don't start."

"Start what?"

"Acting like—my ma, or something."

Laura Strickland

Shock kept Phoebe silent while he ran out, at which point she laid her paint brush aside because her hands shook too badly to hold it.

So apparently she wasn't the only one with an impulse to protect Angus.

He came home about an hour later, by which time Phoebe had given up trying to paint for lack of light.

The rain had become a torrent. He came through the shop doors shedding water, the shoulders of his frock coat darkened and droplets spraying from the brim of his top hat.

Phoebe hurried to meet him. Catching up a shop cloth, she watched as he shrugged from the coat and lifted the hat off with care.

"Raining buckets out there," he said.

"Yes. Here, better take off your shirt, too. You are wet right through."

He focused those mild, blue eyes on her. Only at this moment they didn't appear completely mild.

"Where's Ned?" He glanced at the primer, which Phoebe had rescued from the flood. "He here?"

"Out with his friends. Taking shelter—at the bakery, probably." Stepping up to him, she reached for the buttons on his shirt, a delicate hum starting up inside. Just the two of them here together, with the rain hemming them in. Suddenly it seemed like a world complete.

But he batted her hands away. "Don't touch me."

"I beg your pardon?" Alarm and affront raced through her.

"I've just been handling a corpse."

"Oh." Relief rushed in. "I'm sure you washed up afterward, didn't you?"

"I did. But still, no woman should—"

Phoebe fixed him with a stare. "I'd better inform you, attempting to tell me what I should do rarely ends well. Also, I'm not like other women."

His gaze met hers at last. His voice rumbled in his chest when he said, "Ye've no need to tell me that."

"Well, then. I'm surprised it's even a consideration."

"Miss Phoebe—"

"Master Angus. Hush. If you open your lips again, I fear only dire warnings will come out. Besides, with Ned away and your customers hiding from the rain, we have this place all to ourselves. Do you really want to waste precious time carping at me?"

"I wasn't—"

"I can think of something much better to do."

With that, she leaned up on tiptoe and kissed him.

Chapter Fourteen

Back in the days when Gus endured life beneath the thumb of his old master, Silas Groat, he'd sometimes wondered if he would go mad. It wasn't just the beatings, though they were hard to bear for a young lad alone and away from home for the first time. It was also the things Groat made him do, from washing down the dead—something he rarely thought twice about these days—to sleeping on a narrow cot with nothing more than a thin plank wall between him and the corpses. And Groat's vicious manner when alone with his employees, which could alter to slimy unctuousness when a customer came in.

Eventually, Gus realized he had to get away, if only to save his soul, and even if it meant breaking his contract—and the law. All the same, he was proud he'd endured the ordeal, that his mind stayed strong enough to keep from breaking.

Now, though, he began to wonder if his poor, beleaguered mind hadn't broken its bonds with reality after all. For none of what was happening could be happening.

Life and circumstances had changed him into a practical man. He hadn't always been that way. Back in Scotland, he'd believed in fairies, in boogies and loch monsters. Here, he'd put all that away from him.

Or thought he had.

Yet what occurred after he'd trudged home in the rain must be pure fancy, or a dream.

Because Phoebe—lovely, elegant Phoebe—kissed him. There in the dusty confines of his shop, with the rain drumming on the roof, she bestowed the kind of kiss intended to warm a man right through.

Or to unhinge his mind.

Then she towed him by the hand—a hand she rightfully shouldn't even agree to touch—through to the back room where, as she put it, they could be private together. She finished unbuttoning his wet shirt and pulled it off him before addressing the string vest he wore beneath.

"Strip that off also, Angus."

He stared at her, on a rising wave of heat. Nobody called him Angus. He'd almost forgotten it was his real name.

He obeyed, even while she nipped through to the shop. When she stepped back in, he stood half naked, drying off with the cloth.

"There." Her eyes danced at him. "I've barred the door. No one can come in."

"Why? What ha' ye—" If she told him to remove his trousers, would he obey?

"Why?" she echoed. "So we will not be interrupted."

She hauled the cap from her head and her hair tumbled down, gloriously mussed, just begging Gus to plunge his fingers through. But—those fingers had recently handled a dead cowboy.

Phoebe planted her palm in the center of his bare chest and pushed him into a chair. Before he could blink twice, she perched sideways on his knees, and wound her arms around his neck.

"That's better."

"Phoebe—" This could not be what it seemed. Such things simply did not happen to well-mannered undertakers.

"You are far too tall for me to kiss easily while on your feet. Or perhaps," her eyes danced still more wickedly, "I am merely too short."

Gus went very still. He'd fantasized about this, about having her in his arms, and on his knee. Perhaps he'd died on the way home, and this was what came after.

"I missed you while you were gone," she told him.

"I, uh—" He possessed no slick words, never had. Those he spoke usually came from his heart, which now felt full to bursting.

It didn't matter, because she stopped all words by kissing him again.

She was right—having her here on his knee made things much better. Their lips joined and melded together, and she leaned into him in a confiding manner that allowed him to feel all of what lay beneath the lad's clothing, including a pair of soft, luscious breasts.

Most definitely a dream. One of which he'd truly better take advantage, for dreams were fleeting and—

He plunged his fingers into her hair, completely forgetting where those fingers had so recently been. It allowed him to tip her head back and kiss her more deeply. She parted her lips beneath his, and he drank of her, diving deep. Better than whisky and surely far more intoxicating.

Oh, lord, he was lost.

She wiggled closer, doing dire things to him down

below. Dire and delightful things. Perhaps all women should wear trousers.

She ran her palm up his naked chest and onto his cheek, and kissed him still more enthusiastically.

For several minutes, the only sound in the room was the crashing of the rain on the roof. Then Phoebe sighed and drew back to look at him.

And look she did. Her inspection started at his hair, still wet and half-flattened from the weight of his hat, clung to his eyes, swept over his nose and fastened upon his mouth. Her eyes dilated.

"I missed you, Angus Wright," she repeated, as if it were some kind of vow. "Kiss me again."

He shouldn't. He truly shouldn't. Things had already grown so heated, he'd gone hard for her. Matters, with the two of them alone here together and the door locked, could get out of hand.

Och, and he wanted them to.

While he hesitated, weighing wisdom against desire, she began unbuttoning her shirt, holding his gaze all the while. No mistaking the action. She wanted—she wanted—

As if there remained a question, she grabbed one of his bony mitts and laid it against the soft skin of her breast, for she wore nothing, nothing beneath the shirt.

He snatched the hand away again. "No, Phoebe. I've been handling—"

"You think I mind? You said you washed up, after."

"Aye, but—"

She brought his fingers to her lips and kissed them before placing them on her breast again. Heaven ensued. Gus forgot the rain. He forgot his activities out at the ranch. He damn near forgot who he was. There existed only the warmth of Phoebe in his arms, her incredible softness, the kisses she granted him, and her repeated requests, "Touch me. Touch me, Angus."

He did so most gently, reverently, and with rampant delight. He did not understand why she wanted kisses and caresses from him, of all men. But at that moment he believed she did, and an undiscovered part of him came alive. That part of him, for better or worse, would forever belong to Phoebe Corbet.

She liked it when he palmed her breast, when he thumbed the tight bud at its tip. It made her kiss him as he'd never been kissed before, as if she'd consume him. She liked it even better when he slid his hand down inside the waist of her trousers. It made her wiggle on his lap and stretch like a cat, so he could reach the hot, damp center of her womanhood.

For an instant suspended in time, he gazed at her, lying across his knees, shirt flung open to display those small, plump breasts. Legs spread open, in invitation. Eyes half hooded with passion.

"Touch me, Angus," she begged again.

He thrust one finger inside her. Hot. Wet. A venture into a higher level of heaven he'd never imagined. She reared up and kissed him, even as he worked his fingers inside her and their tongues mingled in a parody of his movements.

And then, she came apart in his hands.

She did so with a gasp into his mouth and a mighty release of tension. He felt the waves of pleasure wrack her and nearly disgraced himself right there in his trousers.

She clung to him while the climax passed, and

after, when she whispered, "Angus? Oh, Angus."

Sanity returned to him slowly. His fingers, still inside her, had experienced what she felt. He withdrew them gently and drew the shirt closed over her breasts.

Embarrassment caused him to look away. Such intimacy, being foreign to him, felt all too strange. "I'm that sorry, Miss Phoebe. By God, I don't know what I was thinking."

"No, it was me. It was all me. You must think me entirely shameless." She drew herself up, rose from his lap, and strove visibly to gather her emotions. "I swear to you, I have never done anything like that before, never even been alone with any man. Nor have I wanted to be."

Gus barely heard her, for the rushing in his ears. "Excuse me." He pushed past her and went out the back, stumbling toward the wee housie.

Half way there, he stopped and let the rain have him, soaking him down and cooling the inevitable steam of his passion.

He'd never imagined he could be capable of such feelings.

What was he to say to her, now that he'd had his fingers in her most intimate of places? What tell her, if he went back inside?

He could never look her in the eyes again.

Better he should go on walking, trudge off this heat that had consumed his sanity.

Before he could move, Phoebe pelted out through the rain to his side. She seized hold of his arm and tugged at him. "Come back in."

"Better not."

"Angus—it's my fault, what happened." Releasing

his arm, she looked up at him. The rain soaked her hair and ran down her face. She'd buttoned her shirt crookedly.

With a vicious bite at her lip, she said, "Perhaps you no longer wish to associate with me."

He wanted to. Truth was, he would like to go back inside and do it all again. His fingers ached to touch her. Parts of him ached for far more.

"It's not that," he said.

"I've embarrassed you."

Aye.

"You think I'm—wanton."

"I do not."

"It's just that I'd missed you and—and I don't know. A madness took hold in my head."

Madness, aye.

"Don't be angry with me."

"I'm not angry." Embarrassed yes, by the intimacy—him not being a man accustomed to such. Terrified by how much he wanted her. Totally at sea as to what to do about it.

Earnestly she went on, "I merely wanted to show you it doesn't matter to me what you do for a living, or what you've touched."

What he'd touched. "I'm goin' for a walk."

"In this terrible rain? Without your shirt? Angus, please come back inside."

"No. Let me be."

She did. She let go of him and stepped away, and he stumbled off into the oncoming evening.

Chapter Fifteen

Things proved awkward the next morning. Phoebe had no chance to speak with Gus when he returned, sodden, from his tramp. It had been very late, and Ned had come home by then.

But she'd had plenty of time to contemplate her recent actions.

What Angus Wright must think of her! In their time together, she'd learned many things of him, among them that he was a true gentleman at heart.

He must be horrified at her bold, shameless behavior.

Indeed, she herself hovered between shock at how she'd behaved with him and a heady kind of bliss. Never, never had she imagined such pleasure as she'd experienced in Angus's arms last evening. Yes, girls thought about what it must be like when men and women were together. She'd learned the facts of life, how babies came into the world. She'd giggled over some of those details with her friends.

None of that correlated in any way with what she and Angus had shared last night. That had been intense and immediate. In all her past imaginings, she'd not allowed for the emotional component. She'd somehow thought it a deed that took place disconnected from feelings.

Not the case. At least, not when it came to being

near Angus. With him, the feelings came first, and unfolded into a passion she couldn't control.

Perhaps, she thought, that was because she felt so safe with him. In his arms, surrounded by his kindness, she allowed herself to let go.

But she had to deal with Angus's feelings, too. This morning, he hadn't been able to look her in the eye. She'd embarrassed him mightily and didn't know how to get back the easy comfort they'd formerly enjoyed.

Especially since, every time she laid eyes on him, she longed to touch him again.

They barely spoke at breakfast. Ned glanced from one to the other of them several times, but didn't ask what had gone awry.

After breakfast, as a watery sunlight burned through last night's rain clouds, Ned ran off to school, leaving the two of them alone. A customer came by, and Gus went out to talk to him, leaving Phoebe alone with Selkie.

Phoebe took up work on Mrs. Standish's sign. But all she could think about was Gus. She'd never hear the sound of rain again without remembering his hand at her breast.

Oh, what was she to do?

He came in quietly and stood watching her at work. She asked, "Did you make a sale?"

"No. He was merely asking about the decorated coffins. How much they cost, and the like."

Striving hard for normalcy, Phoebe said, "I tell you, you're not charging enough."

"People here don't have much to pay. It's not like back where you're from."

She straightened from her work and turned to face him. This time he met her gaze.

"That sign looks beautiful, Miss Phoebe. You are exceedingly talented. Your skill is wasted here."

Was he trying to tell her she should leave? Was he so mortified by what had happened between them, he strove—in his kindly way—to urge her to move on?

She frowned. "You saying Mrs. Standish doesn't deserve a nice sign for her shop? That the folk here in Wylder don't deserve to have pretty coffins for their loved ones?"

"I'm not saying that at all."

She squared her shoulders. "What are you saying, exactly?"

He hauled off his hat, still damp from the rain, and plunged his fingers through his hair. Phoebe's fingers immediately itched. She'd done that same thing last evening, while they kissed—raked his damp mane.

"Miss Phoebe, I'm not good with words, never have been. So I hope you won't take what I'm about to say wrong."

Phoebe braced herself. He meant to tell her she'd behaved like a strumpet. To ask her to leave.

Sure enough, he began, "What happened last night—"

Immediately defensive, Phoebe broke in, "What did happen, Angus? We shared a few kisses."

"You know it went much farther than that."

Her face flamed. "So, I unbuttoned my shirt."

"Farther than that, too. I'm talking about—"

Oh. That. Phoebe couldn't quite say what had happened when he'd touched her so intimately. She'd never imagined her body could respond in such a manner, and the details of it remained lost in the blaze of pleasure.

"Oh," she said aloud.

He shook his head. She expected him to begin talking about what was proper. As she'd learned, his belief in propriety ran deep.

But he said, his voice hushed, "Ye're a beautiful woman. A warm, smart, and—and talented one." He gestured vaguely to the half-finished sign. "How dare ye waste yoursel' on the likes o' me?"

"The likes of you," Phoebe repeated.

"Aye." He tossed his hat down on a chair. "Look at me. Just look."

"I am," Phoebe said, gazing at him steadily.

"I came from nothing more than poverty, back in Scotland. My ma had to barter my future to win me passage to America, and what she thought would be a better life. Despite how hard I've worked, I'm still little better than nothing."

His words were flowing now, sure enough.

"How dare ye throw yourself—and—and your virtue—away on someone of my ilk? I've an ugly past behind me, Phoebe. And there's no reason to believe I'll ever be more than I am now. Someone who knocks together rough wooden boxes. Who handles the dead."

He was indignant on her behalf.

"Angus, I've a past running behind me too. What makes you suppose I'm so much better off than you?"

"Look at ye!" He waved a hand. "Despite the lad's clothing and all your playacting, your quality shines through. Ye should be gracing a grand house some place. You should be pouring tea."

"Pouring tea?"

"You're bright and educated, with talent that's spilling over. Aye, ye've ended up in trouble, and fetched up in this dusty town. That doesn't mean ye belong here, wasting yoursel' on a poverty-stricken undertaker."

"I see." Quite carefully, Phoebe laid her paint brush aside. "Well, Angus Wright, I know little of your past, just as you know little enough of mine. But despite what you say of yourself and your current state of poverty, your quality also shines through. Even more, I should say, than mine. So what are you truly trying to say? That I—a thief and a fugitive—am not worthy of you?"

He stepped toward her and lifted his hands. "Not that."

"Good." She jerked up her chin. "For I know my worth. You, it seems, do not know yours. Yes, things became a bit—heated last evening. I would not want you to believe I'd behave that way with just any man. So you must have some worth, yes, if I chose you?"

"Chose me?" he repeated blankly.

Couldn't he see the truth, the silly fool? That she, Phoebe Corbet, was falling for him, tumbling harder and faster than she'd ever thought possible.

His eyes narrowed. "Since we are speaking plainly here, might I ask you something more?"

She propped her hands on her trousered hips. "I wish you would."

Emotions flickered in his eyes, doubt and something else that she couldn't name. "Last night's events and what happened between us—"

"Yes?"

"Was that just you persuading me to let you stay?"

Her eyes widened. "Is that what you thought?"

"No, not at the time. But it did come to me this morning, when I was searching for reasons why a woman like ye would let me kiss ye that way, touch ye that way with my great, mucky mitts."

"You fool!" This time she said it out loud. "Is that the only explanation you could come up with?"

"It seems the most likely one."

"What about 'I am attracted to you'? I like your 'great mucky mitts.' I like the way you touch me with them. I like the way you kiss me. Does that make me a scheming wretch?"

"Nay, nay." He made soothing motions with his hands. "Keep your voice down. The neighbors will overhear."

"Hang the neighbors. Do I need to show you all over again?"

She stepped up, seized the lapels of his coat in both hands and drew him down within reach. The kiss she planted on him contained all her frustration. It swiftly melted and transformed into heat.

It took Gus several long seconds to respond. Phoebe felt him hold back, fighting his impulses, only to melt in turn.

"By God," he said at last, when the kiss ended and they both breathed raggedly. "What's to be done?"

Phoebe could think of only one thing. It was something she'd never truly contemplated before, not even back in the days when she and her friends giggled over such matters.

She'd always imagined, in some vague way, she would eventually select a man the same way she did a hat or a coat—made of the best material, to last the longest, and worth the cost.

Now her heart had made the leap and chosen in spite of her.

"Let me stay with you, Angus Wright," she told him. "And never, never doubt why I'm here."

Chapter Sixteen

"Tell me about yourself," Phoebe requested.

Gus shot her a look from beneath raised brows. They worked together in the bright sunshine out front of the shop, Gus knocking together another coffin from plain pine boards, and Phoebe putting the finishing touches on Mrs. Standish's sign.

She loved working with him this way, enjoyed the feeling of connection and the deep contentment that possessed her when they were alone together. Even if it did mean she had to keep the cap crammed on over her hair in the hot sun.

Oh, for a bit of rain when he might take her in his arms again.

He mopped his brow. "Nothing much to tell."

He stepped up next to her. Another reason she liked working with him this way lay in the fact that he invariably took off his top hat, so she could see how the sun spun threads of gold in his light brown hair. He also stripped off his coat and worked with his shirtsleeves rolled up, revealing sinewy forearms. Heavens, she couldn't keep her gaze from him.

"That sure is pretty," he said of the sign.

"Do you think Mrs. Standish will be pleased?"

"Don't see how she could be otherwise. She pays up, you keep all of it. You'll need it, for a new start—or for fare back home." Carefully, he added, "Whatever you decide."

And don't you want me to stay? Last night, you made me believe you did. But this morning, he'd made no answer to her appeal. Phoebe didn't quite dare ask the question aloud. Instead she said, "I think we should split it fifty-fifty. You need to save up for a horse and wagon. That way, you won't have to borrow one from the livery for every funeral."

He'd done that just this morning, when he led the cowboy to rest at the Bone Orchard burying yard.

"Buck gives me a good rate. And it's not like we need a hearse, here."

"A hearse?"

He turned back to his task. "In Baltimore, when I worked for Mr. Groat at his undertaking business, he had a great, black wagon with glass sides so you could see the deceased go by on his way to the cemetery. And he dressed us boys up in little black coats with top hats to walk along in front. The horse was black too, of course. For big, important funerals, he'd hire wailers."

"Wailers!"

"Women, mostly, to dress in black and walk along mourning and sobbing into their handkerchiefs. Imagine! They didn't even know the deceased. But it looked good. 'Twas all about how it looked, see?"

Phoebe asked carefully, "And exactly how did you end up with this Mr. Groat?"

Gus did not answer.

"Last night, you said something about your mother signing away your freedom."

"She was a good woman, my ma. I wouldn't want you to think differently."

"I don't imagine anything else."

"She did what she could to give me a chance, one she believed I'd never have in Scotland. After my da died, we had nothing. She worked scrubbing till she got turned away, because her employer had also fallen on hard times. I was only nine, but I worked as I could, for pennies.

"She talked about taking us to the poorhouse. She didn't want me living there, so she indentured me to the captain of a ship bound for America. He paid my passage and so had the right to sell my labor when we reached these shores."

"But—you were only a child."

He gave her a bleak look. "Many are. I was sick for home and missed my ma more than I can say. But when we reached Baltimore, there was Mr. Groat. He liked the look o' me. Fancied I'd be prime, leading his funeral processions, for I was tall even then, if thin as a beam."

"How long was your indenture?"

"Seven years."

"Seven!" Phoebe gasped.

"A young lad doesn't earn much, and it takes a long while to pay off such a debt. As it was, I lasted till I was thirteen. I ran out on the last four years of my contract. So ye see, Miss Phoebe, you're not the only one on the run."

"Oh," Phoebe breathed. "But surely—that was years and years ago. He wouldn't press the matter, still?"

Gus gave a dry laugh. "Silas Groat's no' the man to let bygones be bygones."

"Perhaps you could pay him. Just to be free of it all." Phoebe had learned how terrible it felt, having something like that hanging over one's head.

"Perhaps I could, if I saved hard. But I cannot see Silas Groat being satisfied with mere payment. He sued grieving widows for pennies owed."

"Is that why you're so kind? So—so forgiving? You don't want to be like him."

Gus rested his mild blue eyes on her face. "I've learned from him, perhaps, there are things more important than pennies."

"A valuable lesson to receive." He was, without question, the most decent man she'd ever known. "Was he very cruel to you?"

"Cruel?" For an instant Gus stopped working and stared away into the past. "He was at us continually. Naught we did was ever right, or done well enough. He let his strap do the disciplining."

"Oh." Phoebe flushed with distress on Gus's behalf. "How awful." No wonder he had a low opinion of himself.

"It was that, Miss Phoebe. But I learned a lot, it seems, besides how to be kind. I kept my mouth shut and observed. And I've used what I learned to start my own business." He spread his hands. "So ye might say I've been fortunate."

Not at all. "Did you not think about going home to Scotland?"

"At first, 'twas all I could think about. I wanted naught so much as to see my ma. But it was an impossible goal. I had to get out of Baltimore where old Groat's reach was so long. I had to survive, out on my own. I damned near didn't."

"What made you come west?"

"A good question. I suspect it was fear. No

distance from Groat seemed great enough. And everybody I met kept saying 'twas where a young man could make his fortune. I fetched up here by chance, traveling with a family who since moved on. I stayed."

"In all that time, have you heard from your mother?"

Gus shook his head.

Phoebe's heart clenched. "Not at all? You should have written to her."

"I did. When still I was with Groat, I sent some letters. But I've no idea whether she ever got them."

"She didn't write back?"

"Ma could not read or write, though she made sure I could. She would have had to get someone to read a letter to her, and pen something back to me. She may have gone into the poorhouse, and never got my letters at all."

"Oh, Gus." Phoebe longed to touch him—just a gesture of comfort. But they worked out here in the sun where everyone could see.

Imagine, not knowing what had happened to his mother. Uncertain as her own situation might be, at least she knew her mother remained at home in Cedar Rapids. And Jasper wouldn't harm her. Would he?

Gus shrugged uncomfortably. He didn't want Phoebe's pity. "Somewhere back in Kansas, I decided she's probably dead. She'd want me to make a life of some sort. And I've learned there's no going back again."

Damn it, Phoebe thought in a decidedly unladylike fashion. If only those jewels would turn up, she'd gladly sell them all—cherished designs or not—in order to benefit Gus. She'd buy him that horse and wagon.

Send what he owed back to that old reprobate, Groat. Maybe even take him on a voyage home to search for his mother.

Because he deserved it. And some things were more important than her own welfare.

Chapter Seventeen

"Will you please take Mrs. Standish's sign to her today?" Phoebe asked the next morning when they'd had breakfast and Ned had gone off to school. "It's all finished."

Gus joined her where she stood regarding the sign propped up in the workshop. A little thrill of pleasure ran through him—the same sort he got when he looked at Phoebe. He could no longer so much as glance at her without that happening.

She'd turned the pine boards he'd sanded into a work of art. Fortunately for both of them, she was able to print out the words "Wylder Side Bakery" across the sign, with a magnificent, multilayered cake on one side and a cherry pie with a slice cut out on the other. Flowers splashed everywhere else—only, they weren't merely flowers. The petals, all bright colors, surrounded centers made of tiny biscuits or other confections.

"That's damned clever," Gus told her. "And unique."

He loved the unique. It was one of the reasons he cherished his hat.

"You think so?"

"I do." What a mind the lass had. What couldn't she accomplish, given the chance?

"I hope she likes it." Phoebe slanted a look at him. "You know, I could easily make you a sign for this place. A better one, I mean. The one out there just says *Undertaker*. A bit bare bone, isn't it?"

"I can scarcely put *Wright's* up there. People would be forever stopping by wanting their wheels repaired."

She sighed. "Very well. Will you carry this over to the bakery for me now?"

"I will." An impulse struck Gus, and he strove to examine it dispassionately. Acting on impulse rarely ended well for him. In this case, though, he couldn't resist. "I'll ferry the sign over to the bakery, but why don't ye come with me?"

Her eyes lifted to his. "Should I?"

"I don't see why not." He tugged down the brim of her cap, just for the sake of touching her. "So long as ye keep this on. That way, ye can see how the lady likes her sign."

Phoebe's face lit. "But—folks will see me."

"Those who've been by here already know about you and have accepted ye as a lad." Though God knew how.

"Well, so long as you think it's safe. I can't tell you how I'd like to get away a short while."

"We'll wait a bit, till we're sure she's open."

The sign, some three feet wide by five feet in length, made an armload. Gus carried it painted side out to show off Phoebe's work and couldn't help a stab of pride when folks they met stared in awe. Smiles broke out across their faces. Phoebe, he thought, needn't have worried. No one even seemed to notice her following along.

The bakery was located on the north side of Wylder Street, about half way along, right next to Doc Sullivan's. A good location, it saw a lot of traffic, and since the good aromas drifted out into the street, folks tended to stop in.

Mrs. Standish had pretty, red-and-white checkered curtains at her window, and a tiny table with a checkered cloth. A counter ran across the width of the room, half-filled at this hour with freshly baked goods.

Mrs. Standish came out from the back when they went in. She wore a white apron over her plain skirt and blouse, her white-blonde hair piled atop her head.

A delighted smile appeared on her face when she saw the sign. "Oh, my!" She clasped her hands together. "I didn't expect anything nearly so grand."

Gus smiled too. "We're happy you're pleased."

"Pleased? That doesn't half describe it. What a wonderful job you've done."

"What a wonderful job my assistant has done, you mean." Gus indicated Phoebe with a jerk of his elbow, since he still held the sign.

Mrs. Standish looked at her. "You did all this work, young man?"

"Well, Gus, here, put together the sign."

Mrs. Standish came closer to examine it. "You have an extraordinary talent."

"I keep telling him he's wasted here in Wylder."

Mrs. Standish turned her blue eyes on Gus. "Don't say that, Mr. Wright. Wylder is an up-and-coming place. A grand place to live. Especially with such talented folks as we have settling in."

Briskly, she turned to the counter. "Let me pay you what I owe. And a bit extra for the young artist."

Since Gus's hands were full, she gave the coins to Phoebe.

"I'll ask my husband to take down that old, ugly

sign and put this one up, soon as he's finished at the livery today. I can hardly wait."

In his shy way, Gus offered, "If ye have a ladder, ma'am, I could put this up for ye."

"You do that, Mr. Wright, and there's a big piece of pie in it for you and one for the young man."

Phoebe stood outside and watched while Gus took down the old, weathered sign and hammered up the new one. She enjoyed watching him work because, when he did, he forgot himself and moved with smooth competence.

Other folks stopped to watch also, shoppers and passersby. They murmured in appreciation when the new sign went up. Mrs. Standish came out to take a look.

"Splendid!" she declared. She threw an arm around Phoebe's shoulders and gave her a squeeze. Calling to the crowd, she said, "If anyone wants a grand sign like this one, apply to Wright's undertaker shop. Now, you two come in for your pie."

They sat at the tiny table in the front window, like proper customers. Mrs. Standish set two huge slices of pie in front of them before going out back, to her ovens.

Phoebe's heart rose. "This is fun." It had been far too long since she'd enjoyed anything besides being in Gus's arms.

"Best pie I ever tasted, hands down."

"I agree."

Phoebe glanced outside, where she saw a gentleman standing, just where he could see them through the window. Something about him—his bearing or the way he dressed—caught her attention. Wearing a fine coat of gray broadcloth, he also sported a pair of pistols.

And he stood like a policeman.

Her heart sank, and her euphoric mood evaporated. The pie stuck in her throat.

"Don't look now," she told Gus, "but I think we're being watched."

"Eh?" He glanced out the window. His eyes narrowed. "I've seen that fellow before."

"Where?"

"At the train station. He got off the last train. Not many people do—that's why I remember."

In a whisper, Phoebe asked, "Do you suppose he's come looking for me? Or for Emil?"

"Why would you think that?"

"I don't know." She twitched her shoulders. "Just a feeling I have."

Gus stared at her unhappily.

"Or he could be looking for *the cargo*," Phoebe said.

"I'm sorry," Gus said. "I thought it would be safe to bring you here."

"No, I'm sorry," she returned, "for landing you in all this trouble." He deserved better. She should leave him to his quiet life. Only—only she didn't know if she could, now.

"Finish your pie. Let's get home."

The rest of the pie didn't taste quite so good. The man in the gray suit lingered on the street, talking to townsfolk when they went out. He didn't so much as glance at them, but as they walked away, he headed for the bakery.

"He'll ask Mrs. Standish who we are," Phoebe fretted.

"Aye, and then he'll come looking for us."

****

It didn't take long. At midafternoon, Gus stood talking to a customer, one interested in a sign rather than a coffin. Phoebe worked nearby, sanding another set of boards, when the man strolled up.

Gus noticed the new arrival from the corner of his eye. The customer, who'd seen the sign at the bakery and walked over, just kept on talking. But Gus saw Phoebe glance around and tense, though she refocused her gaze at her job and tried not to let on.

The man in the gray suit eyed the sign on Gus's shop, the one that merely said Undertaker, and then eyed Phoebe. Gus's blood turned cold in his veins.

"Good day, young man," the fellow said.

Phoebe turned her head. She looked so like a woman despite the right-fitting cap, Gus thought surely the jig was up. He thrust out a hand to the would-be customer and said, "Well, Mr. James, as soon as ye come up wi' a design, come on back. I'm sure we can arrive at a fair price."

Well pleased, the customer moved off. Gus turned to the new arrival.

Phoebe had stiffened where she stood, but didn't reply to the man's greeting.

"Can I help ye?" Gus spoke, desperate to distract him.

"Well, I'm not sure. My name is Brice Evans, and I'm an agent with the Pinkerton Agency."

The ice water in Gus's veins stopped flowing. He'd heard of the Pinkertons. Everyone had. In fact, he'd long harbored a fear on some level that old Groat would set them on him. Not that he considered himself important enough for such a pursuit. But here and now, the evil dream came true.

His expression did not change. He'd learned long ago—while marching in one of Groat's funeral processions with the stripes earned in a thrashing still beneath his clothes—to disguise what he felt.

He put out a hand. "Mr. Evans. What can I do for ye?"

Phoebe shot him a sharp glance. She'd already teased him about his accent, claiming it got heavier when he became agitated.

He rolled an eye at her in turn. He would do whatever he could to protect her. He hoped she knew that.

Evans shook his hand, his grip firm. "I'm here in Wylder investigating a disappearance. Looking for a young woman, in fact. I have reason to believe she got off the train here, more than a week ago."

"Oh, aye?" Gus gave him what he hoped was a bland stare. "Disappeared, you say?"

"Yes, and her family back in Cedar Rapids are terribly worried about her. Have you seen this woman?"

From his vest pocket, Evans produced a tintype, which he held out for Gus's perusal. It showed a young woman so elegant that she had little resemblance to the *boy* standing beside him, with sawdust on his hands and mud on his feet.

Much struck, Gus stared. The woman in the tintype stood with one hand resting on the back of a gracefully carved chair, her head poised high on a fragile neck. She wore an elegant, stiffly ruffled dress and an equally fashionable hat upon her hair. Her expression looked composed and refined.

Gus puffed out a breath of relief. No one would recognize Phil in this.

"She's quite lovely." And, as if it needed re-enforcing, too good for him.

Evans grunted. "She's a thief and a runaway, and quite likely in a great deal of trouble. She's capable of spinning wild stories. But you wouldn't be doing her any favors, keeping her from her family."

"I can truthfully say I've not seen a woman so elegant here in Wylder."

"How about your nephew?" Evans, his gaze sharp, tipped the photo toward Phoebe, who stole a look at it.

"Ah, he's not my nephew," Gus said quickly. "Only child, me. Phil is my young cousin."

"Yes? The woman in the bakery called him your nephew."

"She's mistaken. My uncle's youngest, is Phil, come west on an adventure."

Mr. Evans fixed his gaze on Phoebe, who kept her head down. "Traveled by yourself did you, young man? On the train?"

Phoebe nodded and went back to her sanding, all her attention bent on the boards.

"Training with your cousin, are you?" Evans continued pleasantly.

"He hopes to," Gus answered.

"And does young Phil not speak for himself?" Evans asked. "Phil, do you have an accent like your cousin's?"

"Aye, sir," Phoebe croaked.

"The lad has a stutter," Gus said quickly, "and does nae like to speak."

"I see." Evans gave Gus a narrow-eyed stare. "The

woman at the bakery said he helped create her sign."

"Aye."

"A splendid job." Evans' stare hardened. "It is a singular skill, being able to paint so well, especially at such a young age."

"He's learning," Gus said, "and will no doubt improve if he does nae get homesick and return home."

"And where is home, if you don't mind me asking?"

"Baltimore," Gus blurted, and then could have kicked himself. He didn't want this investigator asking uncomfortable questions there.

Evans fished a square of card from his pocket. "Here's my direction. Be sure and contact me if you happen to see the woman in the photograph. Her name is Phoebe Corbet. And, young man—"

Phoebe looked up.

"—good luck with your apprenticeship."

Neither of them so much as breathed while Mr. Evans walked away.

Chapter Eighteen

"He recognized me," Phoebe fretted, and not for the first time. "I know it."

Gus said nothing. They'd retreated inside the shop after the Pinkerton agent left, the better to hash over their dilemma. Phoebe now held the man's card in her hand:

Pinkerton's Agency.
Investigators.
Criminals brought to justice.

She must have read it over a dozen times. Each time, it turned her sick inside.

She fretted at Gus's silence, half frantic. "Why else would he have come straight here from the bakery?"

"I don't know." Gus rubbed at his forehead. He'd removed his hat and set it atop one of the coffins, where it shouted its incongruity.

"Jasper will have told him I'm an artist. That I created the jewelry he's after. This Evans must be searching for the jewels, right?"

"But why should he conclude you got off the train here in Wylder? Of all places."

Phoebe shook her head in turn. "Maybe he's already inquired in Laramie. Maybe he's caught Emil, who told him about me hiding in the casket."

"If that's so, the conductor will have told him Ned and I collected it."

"I'm sure he recognized me."

"I'm not," Gus objected. "If that were the case, wouldn't he have taken you into custody? The conductor, aye, will have told him the casket—in which you may or may not have been concealed—was collected by me and my lad. He'll think you were Ned."

"Or he took a good look, and recognized me."

Gus devoutly hoped not. "You look nothing like the woman in that photo."

"You think not?"

"I do. She is polished and elegant and, och, so very beautiful."

Phoebe stared at him. "Well, thank you very much, Angus Wright."

Her indignant tone made Gus smile as he approached her. "You're also verra bonnie now, if one likes a bit o' grime, and sawdust in the hair."

Phoebe searched his eyes. In the past, she'd never lacked confidence in her appearance. She'd taken for granted that men found her attractive and, in all honesty, had disdained their attention.

Now she wanted but one man to admire her—no, to find her the most desirable woman on earth, despite the sawdust and the grime.

Touch me, she thought, and just as if he heard her, he grasped her shoulders lightly between his hands.

"Need ye ask, lass? You are more lovely than a sunrise."

So poetical were the words, especially coming from this man's lips, foolish tears flooded her eyes.

"Oh, Angus, what are we to do? I fear something dreadful has happened to Emil. He's either dead or has been apprehended. Otherwise, this Pinkerton agent never would have centered his interest on Wylder."

Gus shrugged. "He may be asking questions at every town along the line."

"But then, where's Emil?"

"I have to admit, that's a topper. Try not to worry, lass." He added awkwardly, "Trust I'll look after ye."

"I do trust you, Angus." She went forward into his arms and planted her cheek against his shoulder. It felt so wonderful, despite her worry, she closed her eyes in momentary bliss. She trusted him the way she had no other man, ever. But would their association bring trouble down on him, as it had Emil?

The very last thing she wanted to do.

****

That night, prey to her thoughts, Phoebe could not sleep. Even after Ned rolled into his nest of blankets on the other side of the shop, after she and Gus sat together long, not talking and separate in their thoughts, and after Gus at last went off to bed, she struggled for a measure of peace.

She lay long atop her blankets, arm bent across her forehead, staring into the dark and listening to the not-quite-quiet of a Wylder night. Music drifted down from the Wylder County Social Club, up by the tracks. Voices came from the direction of the saloon, and an occasional horse whickered at the livery.

What was she doing here? How had her life come apart to such a degree that she found herself camped at an undertaker's shop in Wylder, Wyoming?

It felt like madness, all of it—like she'd just awakened from a crazed nightmare to reach for reality. The dispute with Jasper, back home. Her indignation at his treatment of her, and her decision to take back what belonged to her. Mother's choice to confide in Emil, and his offer to help. The entirely unsupportable plan to let him hide her in a casket and escape to the West for a new start.

She'd meant to sell the jewelry, found a business of her own, and send for Mother—free her from Jasper's grasp. A woman, she'd declared, could make her way on her own. This woman would.

Instead, she was hiding out with an undertaker, and had a Pinkerton agent on her tail. Emil might be dead, and her mother lay still in peril—very much *un*rescued.

And she, Phoebe Rose Corbet, had fallen in love with the undertaker.

She scrambled up from her blankets and onto her feet, suddenly too restless to keep still.

Tiptoeing in an effort to keep from waking Ned, who lay curled up in a ball with the raggedy Selkie, she peered out the front window to where bright moonlight lit the street, making it look stark and cold.

How could she have let such a thing happen? She, of all women, who always kept her head and weighed men on their merit. And Angus Wright, of all men.

But—she had done exactly that, hadn't she? Weighed him on his merit. That was the whole point. Her heart had not found him wanting.

She had to stop playing at games, for the situation was deadly serious both for her and for him. Something terrible may have happened to Emil. The jewels might well have been recovered. Which meant Jasper, in sending the Pinkertons after her, was out for revenge.

She knew her stepfather and knew he wouldn't stop, wouldn't rest, till he found and humiliated her.

It was what he did.

She needed to go back home to Cedar Rapids.

But how could she leave Angus?

Very quietly, she let herself outside the front door. The night air felt wonderfully cool. The coffins ranged along the front of the building cast stark moonshadows, narrow and tall. She shivered in reaction.

She hadn't yet saved the full fare to get home. But if she went to the Pinkerton agent and told him who she was, he'd get her back to Cedar Rapids right enough, where she'd face retribution. That would end it, one way or another.

It would remove the danger from Angus's life. Because her problems weren't his problems, and if she cared for him, she'd face the mess she'd made, like a grown woman.

She wanted to be a woman again. She wanted it for him. And herself.

Slowly, she pulled the cap from her head. She could see her own moonshadow on the ground between those of the coffins, and saw her hair tumble down, transforming her into her true self.

A woman should always follow her heart.

That thought took her back inside, her cap still in hand. Selkie lifted her head as Phoebe tiptoed past Ned, who snored lustily, and crept into the back room without a sound.

Moonlight flooded through the rear windows and showed her Angus Wright—asleep.

He looked very young, sprawled in his bed. He had one arm flung out and his cheek turned on the pillow, his hair all tumbled in disarray.

With the lashes long upon his cheeks, he looked like a sleeping angel.

A woman, so Phoebe reflected, couldn't give up what she'd never had, not even for love. And she'd be damned if she would make the ultimate sacrifice without tasting heaven first.

She wore no shoes, having kicked them off to sleep. She tossed down the cap from her hand, and shed the rest of her clothing with alacrity, not giving herself a chance to doubt.

Doubt that he'd want her climbing into his bed, that he'd welcome her company. Just once, before she gave him up for the sake of love.

If she went back to Cedar Rapids, it would be as a changed woman. That much she owed herself.

Chapter Nineteen

Gus dreamed he was back home, in a wee boat on the river Spey. Sunlight burned through the morning mist and glittered off the water all around him. The little skiff cradled him like a sheltering hand, ferrying him to the fish he meant to catch and take home for supper. For once, this night, he and his ma wouldn't go hungry.

The little boat tipped violently as someone climbed aboard. He swiveled his head in surprise.

A woman it was—a most beautiful one. She had long, shiny hair, nearly black in color, and a pair of blue eyes that glowed like sapphires. She also had a pair of breasts that bobbed at him as she slid into the skiff, for she was, quite inexplicably, naked.

"Angus," she called his name. "Angus?"

Ah, but he hadn't had a dream like this in ages. They used to torment him as a youth. He thought he'd conquered such impulses.

But this—this was a grand dream!

"Angus?" she whispered it now. "Do you want me here?"

"Aye. Oh—"

She slid her body up against his and kissed him, effectively stopping any further words, if not thoughts. He knew her then, and protest warred with pleasure inside him, a mighty wave.

"Phoebe?"

"Hush. Hush. We don't want to wake Ned, out there."

Ned, out there. The two of them, in here. No, no, they dare not wake Ned.

He wanted to ask what she thought she was doing. He wasn't fool enough. He knew. He'd felt the attraction between them growing and burgeoning. He didn't know whether the decision to act on that attraction could be counted as a good one.

Did he care?

The bed was barely big enough for two, but that didn't matter because she pressed so tight against him, naked—naked everywhere. He, himself, lay mostly naked in the warm night, wearing only his trews, and skin met skin in raw delight. He plunged his hands into her hair, and they kissed. Kissed and kissed.

Good. A good dream.

"I want you, Angus Wright." She breathed it into his open mouth while her body slid over his, and she climbed on top of him. "Are you willing?"

She must be able to feel that he was, right through his trews. He made an unintelligible sound in response and kissed her still more deeply. He slid his hands from her hair down over her back to her buttocks—ah, wondrous sensation—which he cupped and spread. God, how she fit him. It would be the easiest thing in the world to—

Ah, but what if it wasn't a dream?

Fool. It must be. This couldn't actually be happening. Not with her. Not to him. She left off kissing him long enough to repeat, "I want you, and I mean to have you this night."

"D'ye always get what ye want?"

She appeared to think about that. She trapped his face between her hands and gazed into his eyes by the strained moonlight. "Not by a long chalk. But this time—yes, if you're willing."

Should he argue it? He'd have to be mad. Yet, a gentleman—a gentleman would.

His half-stunned mind scrambled for an answer. "Are ye—are ye…I would no' want to ruin ye."

"You are a good man, Angus. A good man." Was she weeping? "I want it to be you, understand?"

"But—"

She silenced him with another kiss. She must be weeping, because he could taste her salty tears.

God, it wasn't a dream.

"Touch me, Angus," she begged, as she had before. She slid from his body onto the ticking beside him, there within the narrow bed.

"Aye."

Those were the last words they exchanged, the last comprehensible ones, at any rate. Tiny sighs of approval escaped her, and moans. A humming started up in Gus's head that seemed to keep time with his racing heartbeat, and the passion pounding through him. He'd never felt so tender, so trusted, or so powerful.

When he entered her at last, when he filled her completely, he knew it no dream but the holiest event of his life.

After, she clung to him and wept. Unmistakable tears, this time.

His heart plummeted. "Phoebe, lass, why d'ye weep?"

"Because. Because it was so beautiful. And because I love you."

He froze. Ah, God, ah, God, what had she just said? Recovering, he tried to draw away.

"No, don't move." She clasped him more tightly, keeping him inside her.

Wild thoughts surged in Gus's mind. She must be mistaken. It was the passion talking—neither of them could deny the passion. All those feelings stirring up must make her think she had a particular warmth toward him.

Him. An undertaker with nothing to recommend him.

He smoothed the tangled tresses back from her face. "Ah, Phoebe, lass—"

She hiccoughed. "This is when you're supposed to say you love me, also."

"I—"

"But don't worry. It will make it easier for me to leave, if you don't say it."

"Leave? But—"

"You must see, Angus. I have to go back to Cedar Rapids. Take care of things. Face Jasper and make it right."

Gus's mind flailed desperately. "You want to do that?"

"No. I need to."

"You'll come back to me, after? I know I've no right to ask you. I have nothing to offer. I'm little better than penniless."

"That's because you have such a soft heart. You give more away than you take in. Which is why I can't let you pay the price—pay the price for what I've done.

The Pinkertons are relentless. I have to make it right."

"And then," he said again, with more confidence, "you'll come back to me."

"If I can. Jasper may insist on prosecuting me to the full extent of the law, just to make a point."

"Then—then I'll come to you. I'll come with ye. Or—or we'll go somewhere else and start a new life."

"Leave Wylder, and all you've built here?"

"What have I built?" Desperation gave the words an edge.

"A business, a good one. Folks trust you. If you can't see that—"

"It all pales beside being with you."

"You do love me. That's all I need to know."

"I love ye, lass. More than my own life. Certainly more than the life I've made here."

"Then show me. Show me again."

They made love frantically, desperately, two souls at sea and going under for the third time. After, she lay draped across his chest, and he stared into the sifted moonlight, because he'd forgotten to consider what Ned might have heard in the room beyond.

He'd forgotten to remain quiet. He'd forgotten everything except the woman in his arms.

He tried to imagine what the morning would bring, and failed. His mind couldn't stretch past this moment.

"Do ye suppose Neddie heard us? What the hell will he think?"

"I'm pretty sure Ned knows the truth, that I'm not a boy."

"Eh?"

"It's just a matter of time till everybody figures it out. That's why," she drew a breath, "I have to turn myself in to that agent, come morning."

"Are ye sure?"

"Yes. I have to see it through, set things right. Find out what's happened to Emil."

He would lose her. Suddenly, Gus knew it for truth, clear as the tolling of a bell. She'd disappear back into her world of fashionable clothes, fine carriages and—and jewels, by God. She'd forget this dusty town and the string bean of an undertaker to whom she'd gifted her virtue one remarkable night.

Perhaps it was a dream after all.

And—and maybe that was for the best. Because, surely, she deserved far better than Angus Wright.

"Trust me," she whispered against his lips. "Trust me, and kiss me again."

Chapter Twenty

Outside, men put up banners across the street, and strung bunting. Folks called to one another merrily, and a cool breeze chased little dust devils underfoot. The wind smelled of autumn and change.

Phoebe, standing in her trousers and her short coat, stared at the scene in disbelief. She squinted at the banner now decorating Wylder Street—*Founder's Day!* in huge letters, red on white. A big do, it seemed. One for which she'd no longer be in town.

She looked at the square of cardboard clutched in her hand. She needed to find Mr. Evans as quickly as possible, because she'd left Angus sleeping. He wouldn't remain asleep for long, not if he became aware of her absence.

Indeed, she could almost feel him even now, stirring.

The banner fluttered just past Wylder's Mercantile. Phoebe stood beside the Wylder Side Bakery, trying to gird her loins for what she must do.

Mrs. Standish came hurrying out of the bakery, ushering ahead of her a boy about Neddie's age, who could only be her young brother. He had the same white-blond hair and clutched a strap of books. After she hugged him and saw him on his way down the street, she glanced at Phoebe in some concern.

"Young master Phil, good morning. Is everything

all right?"

Phoebe shoved the Pinkerton man's card into her pocket and nodded at the banner. "What's that all about?"

Mrs. Standish followed her gaze. "Founder's Day? A big celebration, apparently, not unlike the Independence Day one. I haven't been in town long enough to experience the fun, but I'm assured there's a dance, contests, and good things to eat."

Her blue gaze turned shrewd as it examined Phoebe's face. "Did you come for a biscuit?"

Phoebe shook her head.

"Why don't you come inside and sit down for a moment? Quite frankly, you appear a bit unwell."

"I can't. I'm looking for that Pinkerton fellow."

"Why? Are you in trouble?"

"I need to turn myself in. For—for Angus's sake."

Cissy Standish took her arm. "Here, my dear," she whispered, "come sit down."

Shock, as much as anything, made Phoebe go along with her. Mrs. Standish sat her at the same little table where she and Gus had enjoyed their pie. When Mrs. Standish tried to step away, Phoebe caught her arm in turn.

She gave the woman a searching look. "You know, don't you? That I'm not—"

"A boy? Of course."

"What gave me away?"

Mrs. Standish bit her lip. "A number of things. How well you paint. An extraordinary talent for a young lad. The way you hold yourself. And then—the way you and Mr. Wright looked at each other. Also, you are a bit pretty for a boy."

Tears flooded Phoebe's eyes. "I love him so very much. Angus, I mean. That's why I have to turn myself in to—"

"The Pinkertons?"

Phoebe nodded miserably.

"Let me get us some tea. We'll talk about it."

****

They sat together at the little table in the front window with the sunlight streaming in while people passed by. Customers frequently entered the shop. When they did, Cissy Standish rose and waited on them, her manner friendly and yet somehow dignified.

Proud, that was it, as Phoebe eventually identified. Cissy was proud of her little bake shop and her life here, humble as it might be.

Those who stopped in complimented her on the sign. She smiled and nodded in return, not drawing Phoebe to their attention.

In between, they sat with their heads close, while Phoebe told her story.

"Incredible," Cissy breathed when she finished. "I thought I was a black sheep when I arrived in Wylder."

"I'm not a black sheep, I'm a criminal. A thief. And—and Angus deserves so much better."

"I doubt he'd agree with you."

"But I've ruined his life," Phoebe wailed.

"That's what Buck, my husband, said back after we met. He thought the best thing he could do for me was get out of my life. He was wrong. You know, Wylder's a strange kind of place, one where folks tend to find one another for better or worse. I think there might be a little magic in the air."

"You do?"

Cissy nodded. "I'm not saying you shouldn't go back and rescue your mother. She can't possibly be happy with this vile Jasper character."

"The scales have fallen from her eyes."

"But then you'll have to face the music, so to speak."

Phoebe nodded miserably. "And I can't rid myself of the feeling that if I travel back East I'll never see Angus again."

"Nonsense. He's not about to let you disappear from his life."

"How can you be so sure?"

Cissy nodded out through the window. Following her gaze, Phoebe beheld an outlandish figure, lit by the morning sun. Tall and thin, lithe with whipcord strength, he wore his dusty black coat and the fantastical top hat, as singular an identifier as one of her signs.

"A man doesn't come looking for a woman if he's ready to let her walk out of his life," Cissy said.

Phoebe went out and met Angus in the street. She didn't dare touch him, with so many people on hand to behold the spectacle, but she wanted to.

He looked relieved to see her. "You ran out on me."

"I'm sorry. I thought it best."

"You haven't found that Pinkerton man yet?"

She shook her head.

"Good, because I've been thinking. There must be another way out o' this. One that won't put you in danger."

"I'd rather place myself in danger than endanger you, Angus Wright."

His gaze softened. "Listen to me, lass. I've come up wi' a plan. I have to admit, it's a wild one, and I'm not at all sure it will work."

"Ah?" Phoebe questioned him with her eyes. "But then, sometimes wild plans are the very best kind."

"Aye, well—the first thing we must do is hold a funeral."

****

The coffin was a plain pine box, not one of the decorated units Gus would have preferred to use. He reasoned it would not make sense for him to waste a valuable model on a stranger. But it was well-sanded and flawlessly fitted, the best he could offer the woman he loved.

He might as well admit how much he loved her, something he'd scarcely dared to do even in his own mind. She said she loved him, too—had come right out and spoken the words. He could only hope it hadn't been impulse or stirred emotions talking, given what they'd been up to at the time.

The two of them together loaded the coffin onto the old push cart and shoved it out along the lonely trail to the Bone Orchard Cemetery. Clouds began to gather before they got there, and continued to thicken up the whole time he dug the grave.

"You know," said Phoebe, who'd taken a turn with the shovel but soon handed it back to Gus once more, "it's a strange and uncanny feeling, watching someone dig your grave."

"So I imagine it must be." Gus had taken off his coat and rolled up his sleeves. He dug steadily, as befit such a task.

"I guess, in a way, I'm burying my past."

He shot her a look. "If this works." With every spade full of dirt, it seemed less likely. "You sure that's what you want?"

"Well, I don't like the fact that word may get back to my mother before I'm able to contact her. It will break her heart."

"Aye."

"Though she might already believe I'm dead."

"That's what the Pinkerton man's come to discover."

The first drops of rain hit Gus's back as they slid the coffin into the grave. It came harder and faster while he filled it in, and they pushed the cart home in a downpour that wetted them both to the skin.

"Washing away our sins," Phoebe observed.

"Perhaps so. You realize we're going to have to bring Ned in on the secret."

"I told you, Ned already knows about me."

"Then perhaps he won't be too disapproving."

"Or too shocked when I move into your bed."

Their eyes met for a long moment that contained a battle of wills. "Ah, hell," Gus said. "I'll not win this argument, will I?"

"Not a bit of it. And," Phoebe gained enthusiasm, "I'll need to choose a new name, won't I? To go with my new identity. Since Phoebe Corbet is dead."

"You're right."

"I need something fitting. What was your mother's maiden name?"

"MacGinty. But I'll no' sleep with a woman who calls herself after my mother."

"Very well then. I'll use a name that reflects this wild undertaking of ours, and the chance we're taking.

Fortune. And I'll use my middle name with it—Rose. How does Rose Fortune sound?"

"Rosemary sounds better."

"Rosemary it is. Here, Master Wright." She put out her hand. "Shake on it."

He did, his bony fingers enfolding hers tenderly. What was she made of, this woman who'd claimed his heart? Equal parts seduction and daring, with just enough idiosyncrasies to take her off the rutted road and appeal to the same part of him that treasured his battered top hat.

"Now," he reminded her, "we need to get certain critical members of the town on our side."

She gave him a blinding smile. "So we do."

Chapter Twenty-One

Ned listened to their tale with rolled eyes and a longsuffering expression. "I'm no fool," he said when Gus's rather long-winded explanation ended. "I could see the way you two looked at each other. And, no offense, miss, but you do make a poor excuse for a boy."

"I guess I'll take that as a compliment."

"But it's a mad scheme. You really think you can convince this Pinkerton fellow? And what about your ma? She'll think you're really dead."

"I intend to write her a letter. She'll recognize my handwriting, but I don't think Jasper will, if he sees the envelope. Hopefully, she'll be able to come and join us here."

Ned rolled his eyes again. "Another female? Gus, you're gonna need a proper house."

"You're right." This whole situation, so Gus decided, had turned into the theater of the impossible—or the absurd.

But then, perhaps there'd always been a part of him that desired the absurd, craved it even while he strove to walk the straight and narrow. He'd been boxed into his staid, ordinary life. And maybe that was what attracted him so irresistibly to Phoebe.

Or maybe not. For, once Ned ran off to school, she looked him in the eye and said, "Angus, go lock the door."

"Eh?"

She whipped the cap from her head and moved into his arms. The gleam in her deep blue eyes told him what she wanted.

"But, woman! We've work to do. Ye've a letter to write."

"I don't care."

"And," he objected again, "it's broad daylight."

"The broader, the better." She kissed him and any remaining shreds of good sense flew out of his head.

"Ye're mad entirely," he whispered, just before she went and locked the door with her own hands.

"Aye, Angus." She mocked him with a gentle reproduction of his accent. "Isn't that what love does to a woman?"

Gus had no answer for that, but an hour later he could testify as to what it did to a man—wrung him out dry, and took him to heights so lofty he could glimpse heaven.

Lying like one of his own customers in the narrow bed, he felt her lips trace his jaw before she whispered in his ear, "Um, nice."

He found he could move after all, enough to wrap his arms around her and cuddle her tight. Indeed, he'd rather die than lose her now. He supposed he should tell her so.

But her agile mind leaped ahead. "We have to come up with a back story for Rosemary Fortune—a convincing one. She can't just suddenly appear from thin air."

"The way you did?" He caressed her naked back tenderly. Strength and softness.

"Have I mentioned how much I like the way you touch me?"

With his big, corpse-familiar hands…he didn't mention that, not wishing to ruin such a beautiful moment.

"We've been telling everyone I—Phil—is your cousin. I think Rosemary should be Phil's sister. That way, nobody will think it strange that I might look a little like him, or carry on with the painting."

"That's a cockeyed story, lass. No one will buy it, though ye do look a lot like that Phil."

"I'm his sister."

"But ye won't be seen arriving on the train."

"Neither was Phil."

True.

"And," Gus protested without thinking, "am I to marry my own cousin?"

She went suddenly very still. "Who said anything about marriage?"

Gus experienced a wave of heat, followed by cold. They gazed into one another's eyes, in the gloom.

"Well," he said, sounding like a man who'd just been punched in the gut, "I thought—"

She'd said she loved him, hadn't she? Announced it out in a declaration. And she was talking about staying with him. Didn't that mean they'd wed?

Her voice also sounded a bit strange when she said, "I'm not at all certain I'm the marrying kind."

Or—the thought leaped to Gus's mind—maybe she didn't think he was worth wedding.

And she was right. What woman of her ilk, beautiful, well-educated, and familiar with a wealthy existence, would waste herself on the likes of him?

He didn't deserve her. He didn't warrant *forever*.

The euphoria conjured by their tender lovemaking drained away like rainwater down a gully. Fool. What had he been thinking? The word *love* meant little. And having been alone most his life, it was perhaps his destiny.

"Angus?" She spoke softly. "What's the matter?"

"Well, just that ye've been talking about a new life. I mistakenly thought—"

"Rosemary Fortune will start a new life. Here, in Wylder."

So what was he, Gus, meant to be to her? A leg up? A stepping stone into that life? Was she merely using him after all? Was lovemaking the coin she paid to persuade him to risk everything in order to help her?

He hated that thought and didn't want to believe it. But as he lay there listening to the sounds of a busy afternoon outside, and Phoebe's even breathing after she fell asleep on his chest, he couldn't keep the thoughts from pounding at him.

They felt an awful lot like old Groat's fists.

****

Something, so Phoebe could tell, was very much the matter with Angus, and she feared she knew exactly what.

Ever since their lovemaking in the tiny back room yesterday afternoon, he'd been—well, different. That was when they'd discussed details of their plan to transform young Phil into Rosemary Fortune.

Even though he'd been the one to come up with it, he might have reconsidered the plan. No question, a great deal of the responsibility for carrying it out fell on him. He'd have to lie, and persuade others to lie also. It could cost him dear, in the end.

Or maybe...maybe that wasn't it at all. Perhaps he'd decided she was brazen for throwing herself at him the way she had in the middle of the afternoon. Deep beneath his kind surface and despite his quirky leanings, he was very much the straight-laced gentleman. Had he concluded she wasn't enough of a lady for him?

That thought took her breath away. She could barely make herself contemplate it. Yet she must. She was about to give up her former life in order to be with him. She very much gambled it was what he wanted.

A new future, with her.

Now, as they walked to Doc Sullivan's office, she gnawed on her nail, and wondered. Rarely was she indecisive. But look where throwing herself at things had got her this time.

Into trouble. And Angus Wright's arms. But for how long?

She stole a look at him. He'd been quiet. Well, Gus usually was quiet, on the whole, but this felt different. Worst of all, he avoided meeting her gaze.

"Angus, do we need to have a talk?"

He looked startled. "Now?"

"As good a time as any. We can turn right around and go back to the shop, if you don't like the plan for what we're about to do."

"It's not the plan. It's—"

The front door of Doc Sullivan's office opened. The man himself gazed out into the bustling street. "Morning, folks." His bright green gaze moved over each of them, taking extra time with Angus's hat and Phoebe's face, before his lips quirked. "Something I can do for you?"

Phoebe returned his look with interest. A fine-looking man was the doctor, and no mistake. And sharp as a tack, she was willing to bet.

She said, "If we might have a few minutes of your time, we'd sure appreciate it."

His smile widened. "Sure—son. Come on in."

Chapter Twenty-Two

Doc Sullivan, so Gus reflected a short time later, had been surprisingly easy to persuade. Of course Coyote, as some people called him, was no ordinary doctor. Folks said he'd been through the horrors of the war between the states before coming out west. And he packed a gun, like no physician Gus had ever seen. Had a dangerous air about him.

He'd seemed amused more than anything by their tale. Had that led him to agree? Or was the good doctor, like everybody else in Wylder, just a bit—well, cracked?

Either way, Gus should feel happier about it. Phoebe seemed happy enough, and prattled about Doc Sullivan's virtues while they walked away.

Gus, on the other hand, had settled into a gloom that rivaled what he'd entertained while surviving under Groat.

With a shake of the head, he mumbled, "I can't believe he agreed."

Phoebe glanced at him. "Why?"

"It's a mad scheme."

"Maybe he just believes in true love."

Gus bent a look on her that caused her to pause in the street and prop her fists on her hips. "What's the matter with you, Angus Wright?"

"We still have to persuade Sheriff Hanson, and that

148

may not be so easy. In fact, here's where it can all blow up in our faces."

"You worried about getting arrested?"

"Not me. You might be, though—for theft. I don't know much about the sheriff. If he's a straight law-and-order man…well, I'm sure he's already heard that Pinkerton's story." Sheriff Hanson could clap Phoebe in irons. Put her behind bars.

Gus might never see her again. Which led him to the question—was he better off taking what time he could with her, while she deigned to stay with him? Or having her not at all?

The answer made his heart hurt.

Phoebe didn't shift from her stance in the street. A fellow on horseback had to edge around her.

"You sure nothing more is bothering you?"

"More?" Gus gave a grim laugh.

"Maybe," she hazarded, "maybe you don't want me to stay with you."

"And maybe," he returned, "ye do nae truly wish to stay."

She flushed scarlet. "Why would you say that?" She reached for his arm and he drew it behind him.

"Nay, not here in the street where everyone can see."

"You are right. Tell me one thing, though. Do you want to talk to the sheriff, or do you want to call this off?"

For the span of twenty heartbeats, Gus's good sense warred with his longing while he wondered, what would he do if she did leave him? It would crush him beyond endurance. Yet he had so little to offer her.

"Well?" Challenge flashed in her eyes.

He rose to it. "Let's go talk to the sheriff."

It being early morning, Sheriff Hanson was in. He sat at a desk in the main room of the jail house, which felt cool at this time of day. There were two cells behind him, but both were empty. A second, younger man leaned over the desk, receiving orders. He straightened as they came in, and Gus saw he wore a deputy's star.

Sheriff Hanson had to be in his mid-fifties and had gone gray. The length of his grizzled side whiskers rivaled Gus's own. Even his hat, resting on the desk, had seen better days. But he had keen blue eyes that argued he'd seen a lot and was nobody's fool.

Question was, did he have a heart, also?

He stared at Gus and Phoebe while a rueful expression crossed his face. "Morning. Mr. Wright, ain't it? Isn't every morning the town undertaker comes strolling in. Not something amiss, is there?"

"No, sir. That is, we hoped for a word."

Hanson glanced at his deputy, who'd gone a bit pale. "Uh, Earl," the man stammered, "I'll just go follow up on that matter we discussed. Right?" Some folks felt superstitious about Gus.

"Right," Hanson told the man.

After he went out the door, the sheriff fixed Phoebe with a stare. "Shouldn't you be in school, young fella? Classes started up again last week."

"Well," Phoebe replied, "that's what we wanted to discuss." She pulled the cap from her head and her hair fell down around her shoulders in rich, dark tresses, making Gus's fingers tingle with longing.

Sheriff Hanson's eyes bugged out for an instant before narrowing to slits. "Well, I'll be damned."

Gus glanced nervously at the door and hissed at Phoebe, "Whist! Put that back on. You don't know who will come in."

She stuffed the cap back on her head, will-he-nil-he, leaving some of the tresses free. Hastily, Gus tucked them up inside the fabric, a procedure Sheriff Hanson watched with some interest.

"Sit down, folks," he said, no longer looking sleepy. Slowly, he rose and, limping a bit as if stiff in the knees, locked the door before stumping back to his seat.

Proving his wits moved more quickly than his limbs, he asked, "Well, young—er—lad, would you be the Miss Phoebe Corbet that Mr. Evans, the Pinkerton agent, has been asking about?"

Phoebe and Gus both stared in consternation. Maybe, Gus thought again, this was a bad idea—a very bad idea indeed.

Doc Sullivan, himself recently married, had been sympathetic to their story and, Gus suspected, more than a bit entertained. Sheriff Hanson, on the other hand, didn't appear to have a romantic bone in his body. Plus, as sheriff, wouldn't he be duty bound to hold Phoebe and turn her over to his fellow lawman? Och, what had he been thinking? He was going to lose her one way or another.

Phoebe lifted her head in a queenly gesture. "Yes, I am Phoebe Corbet, and I am on the run. Let me tell you why."

Sheriff Hanson listened. Gus had to give him that. The only time he looked away from Phoebe's face was when he glanced at Gus as if to say, can you believe this? The hard, discerning expression in his eyes didn't change, not even when Phoebe expressed her doubts about Emil's welfare.

When at length Phoebe finished, saying, "You see, I have put Phoebe Corbet to rest and intend to start a new life here in Wylder," the sheriff let out a gusty sigh and rubbed his face with his hands, like a man in pain.

"So, let me get it straight. You expect me to go along with this wild—and, I might add, foolhardy—scheme o' yorn?"

Gus, dismayed, spoke for the first time. "It's a lot to ask, I know."

"It certainly is. She," Hanson pointed at Phoebe, "is a wanted woman, though I'll admit, she scarcely looks it."

"But," Phoebe repeated earnestly, "I didn't steal anything. Those pieces were my own property—sort of. And I don't even have them," she wailed. "They've been stolen."

Hanson leveled a stare on her. "Well, let's take those statements apart, shall we, and look at 'em. Even if I believe all this gobble-de-gook you're feeding me, that you designed that jewelry, you used your stepfather's stock o' gems to do it. Is that right? So there's some question as to whom they truly belong."

Phoebe's mouth fell open.

"As for the fact that the pieces are missing, you're responsible—and answerable—for that also."

Indignant now, Phoebe flared, "I do not know where that jewelry is. It may be back in Jasper's hands by now, if he or his agents apprehended Emil."

"If that were the case, Miss Corbet, why would he go to the expense and trouble of sending a Pinkerton agent after ya?"

"For the sake of vengeance. I told you, he's not a very nice man. He'd go to the ends of the earth to get back at me." She leaned forward in her chair. "Sheriff Hanson, that's why I had to bury Phoebe Corbet. Don't you see? He'll never stop coming after me unless he believes I'm dead."

"So." Hanson fixed her with a hard blue stare. "You want me to lie to a fellow lawman? To drag him out to that burying ground, stand him above some empty grave, and tell him I know for a fact that a Miss Phoebe Corbet lies there?"

Color flared and faded in Phoebe's face. "I don't expect it, Sheriff. But I am hopeful."

"Why should I do such a dab-blasted foolish thing?"

"For the sake of love?" Phoebe clasped Gus's hand. "I love this man, Sheriff Hanson. I want the chance for a new life with him."

Gus's heart leaped and started beating double time. But the sheriff scowled forbiddingly.

"You think I'd perjure myself so you can take up life here in Wylder and marry an undertaker with—forgive me, Mr. Wright—not much more than an outlandish hat to his name?"

"I want to stay here with him, yes." Phoebe hesitated a moment. "I never said anything about marrying."

Even as Hanson glared, Gus's heart fell once again. Hanson had sized him up fairly well. No wonder Phoebe refused to consider marrying him.

A sharp battle of wills ensued. Phoebe stared at the sheriff, and he glared back at her from a face like a thundercloud.

Here it comes, Gus thought. He's going to arrest her on the spot, call for that Pinkerton agent, and let him drag her away, back East. Gus's life would return to existing on what little he could earn, and occasional kindness to strangers. No more watching Phoebe at her work. No more catching her brilliant smile. No warm, loving nights.

Had he truly supposed it could end any other way, for him?

Quite suddenly, the sheriff's tense expression cracked. It broke up into a smile, like sunshine coming through the heavy clouds. He chuckled and started to laugh. He laughed until tears ran down his face, and he slapped the top of his desk.

"Damn it!" he wheezed at length. "Excuse me, miss, but that's the funniest thing I ever heard."

Gus and Phoebe exchanged glances.

More softly now, Phoebe ventured, "Sheriff? Does this mean you'll help us?"

"Fool that uppity Pinkerton agent, you mean? Hell, yes. Fellow's a right snooty customer, thinking he's better than the law here in Wylder. Anyway..." His bright gaze moved from Phoebe's face to Gus's. "Who am I to stand in the way of true love?"

Chapter Twenty-Three

True love.

Those words echoed in Gus's head later that afternoon when the four of them—he, Sheriff Hanson, Doc Sullivan and the Pinkerton agent—stood above Phoebe Corbet's supposed grave.

A small wind blew across the wide expanse of the burying ground, stirring up dust devils here and there from the exposed soil. It felt cold to Gus, like autumn coming, or maybe even winter.

He wore his hat, since he stood more or less in his official capacity. The others had removed theirs. The doc looked somber, and Sheriff Hanson watchful.

Mr. Evans appeared suspicious.

Phil, of course, hadn't come. No reason to draw him to Mr. Evans' attention.

The man needed no encouragement. He glanced from the bare-earth grave to the doctor, who stood rocking on his heels, to Sheriff Hanson. Lastly, he turned his gaze on Gus.

"You expect me to believe you buried an anonymous woman at your own expense?"

"Well, now." To Gus's surprise, Sheriff Hanson spoke up. "Undertaker, here, will be reimbursed. Town has a fund for taking care of unknowns. And she was an unknown when she went in the ground." He asked Gus, "Right, son?"

Gus pried his tongue from the roof of his mouth. He didn't lie convincingly, never had, and feared he'd be the weak link now, in this unlikely consortium of three.

"I never like burying anybody without a name. But yes, I gave her a coffin. It's my job."

"Huh!" Evans glared at him. "And you buried her, when? This grave looks mighty fresh."

Doc Sullivan spoke up. "Look around you. Many of these graves don't grow grass for a considerable length of time."

Evans cast a disparaging look around the cemetery before turning back to Gus. "You say she showed up in a coffin you collected? And it didn't occur to you to report her death?"

"Aye, sir. I did report it to the doc and the sheriff. Didn't know whom else to inform, since we didn't know who she was."

"Did you report it to the railroad?"

"Why should I, sir? They just shipped Mr. Randolph's casket, and they did deliver that safely to me. Not their fault, what came nailed up inside."

Mr. Evans grunted in apparent disapproval. "And you didn't think to mention this to me, when I came asking you and your young cousin about a missing female? When I showed you that portrait of the very same woman?"

Gus drew a breath. "Sir, you said you were looking for a runaway, a living woman—not a dead one. Why should I connect her with a corpse? To be honest," he swallowed convulsively, "she didn't look much like your portrait, after several days in that casket. Just occurred to me after, like, when I got to thinking about

156

it. I did wonder if she could be the woman you were searching for, because of all that black hair. So I went to the sheriff, who called in Doc Sullivan, here."

Evans looked like he wanted to swear. "And her cause of death?"

Gus gave him a wide-eyed stare. "I'm not qualified to say, sir."

His face now expressionless, Doc Sullivan spoke up. "I examined the young woman's remains, Mr. Evans. It's my opinion she smothered. That casket lid was nailed down when Mr. Wright, here, received it."

"So you're saying somebody shut her in there— nailed her in there—and left her to die?"

"Can't say that." Sheriff Hanson drawled. "Well, the first part's pretty certain. Poor girl didn't hammer herself inside that coffin, did she? Whether or not the intention was to kill her or it was an accident…well, who can say?"

Just accept the story, Gus begged the Pinkerton man silently. Take it back to that bastard Jasper Dent, and convince him Phoebe's dead. And buried, like Gus's own past.

Instead, Evans turned to Sheriff Hanson. "Did you report this to anyone back East?"

"Like who?"

"Well, the casket company, maybe."

Sheriff Hanson stared. "You think they put 'er in there?"

"No, probably not. But—well, the authorities in Cedar Rapids should be informed. Someone is looking for her. She has a family."

"Mr. Evans, there are a lot of stops between here and wherever that casket got loaded. Who's to say when she got put in?"

Evans looked livid now. He scuffed a toe in the dust of the grave, like he wanted to uncover the coffin and look inside.

He grumbled, "I find this difficult to believe, gentlemen. A young woman is put into a casket, the lid nailed down—she'd make a fuss, wouldn't she? Somebody would hear her beating on the inside of the lid, crying out."

"If she could." Doc Sullivan put in. "If she wasn't unconscious, or drugged."

Hanson contributed, "Shut away in the baggage car—" He leaned forward to look at Gus. "You did say you received the casket from the baggage car, Mr. Wright?"

Gus nodded. "And this was a quality casket, made solid. The lid was padded with satin. I don't know that anyone would have heard her."

Looking frustrated, Evans drew a notebook and pencil from his pocket. "Description?" he demanded of Gus.

"Eh?"

"What did this dead woman look like?"

"Well, that's what got me thinking about that portrait you showed me, of the beautiful young lass, like an angel. This dead woman was also young. Had— well, the same black hair. As I say, after a wee bit o' decomposition, there's where the resemblance ended."

All three men stared at him. "Color of her eyes?" Evans asked.

"Sir, I didna pry them open to look."

"I did, when I examined her." Doc Sullivan cleared his throat. "They were blue."

Mr. Evans jotted the information down. "You do realize her family will have to be informed. Her mother is going to be devastated by this news."

Gus gave his practiced bow, learned so long ago from Silas Groat. "Please give her my most sincere condolences. And—what did you say she was called?"

"Why do you want to know?"

"I keep a record of everyone I put in the ground on behalf of the town. It's a sad thing, sir, when I have to write down *unknown*."

"Phoebe Corbet. But don't bandy that about, please."

Gus gave another bow. "You can be sure it will stay confidential among us four. In my business, sir, a man learns to be discreet."

"Well," Sheriff Hanson spoke up, "no sense standing out here in the wind. Glad we could put a conclusion to your case, Mr. Evans, but I have other work to do."

"As do I," Sullivan concurred. "Office hours."

Gus put out a hand to him. "Thank ye for your assistance. And you, Sheriff Hanson."

They shook all round.

"Sad set of circumstances," Hanson commiserated. "But no worse than some you've seen, I'll wager, Mr. Wright."

"That is quite true, Sheriff."

The sheriff grinned at him. "At least we can rest easy in the knowledge that this young lady was safe in your hands."

****

Something was still bothering Angus. That truth had been impressed upon Phoebe ever since he'd taken the Pinkerton man out to her grave yesterday. He just wasn't the Angus she'd come to know and love.

Of course, it couldn't be easy, lying to that Pinkerton agent or standing above what was supposed to be her final resting place. But what if Angus experienced regrets?

Regrets about their relationship.

Granted, it had been whirlwind, from the moment he'd lifted her out of that casket to the first time she'd joined him in his bed. The whole thing seemed mad when you looked squarely at it, and she wondered what had got into her head.

Into her heart.

She, who'd spurned suitors on general principle, preferring to remain under her own direction, had tossed even common sense aside over a tall, lanky undertaker with soulful eyes.

She, who'd intended to retain her virtue indefinitely if necessary, had fallen over herself to gift it to him. She'd chucked away her old life—well, that was no great shakes—to take up another here in this dusty western town, as Rosemary Fortune.

Did he have doubts? About her, about his own feelings? By heaven, she could scarcely blame him—she should have doubts also.

But, curiously, she didn't. She'd known what she wanted from the moment she laid eyes on him. No, when she'd learned what a kind soul lay beneath that outrageous exterior, and had seen him smile for the first time.

She wanted to be with him, to stay with him—fully, wholeheartedly, and for good.

But she'd forced him to bend his honor, so deep

and strong within him. And now she didn't know if he wanted her to stay.

Last night, following his trip to the graveyard, they'd slept in the same bed, but he'd barely touched her. Quite an accomplishment, in the narrow cot.

Now they sat together in the tiny back room, in near silence. Phoebe ached to talk it all out—for better or for worse—but Angus, barely communicative at the best of times, looked like he wanted to hold his silence.

Far more brightly than she felt, she said, "The Pinkerton man left on today's train."

"So Sheriff Hanson told me."

Gus had been off and about a lot today. Phoebe wondered if he'd been avoiding her.

She shuffled her chair closer to his and rested her chin on her hand, studying him. His hair gleamed golden-brown in the lantern light. His deep-set eyes revealed little.

"What?" he asked after several minutes. "Have I a smut on my nose?"

"No. You have a very nice nose."

"It's a bony beak."

"It's fine and high-bridged, and lends you character."

He eyed her carefully and gave no opinion.

Judiciously, she went on, "With Mr. Evans gone, I'm thinking it's time for Rosemary Fortune to put in an appearance. How would it be if you put your cousin Phil on the next stage—I've a bit of Mrs. Standish's money set aside for that—for everyone to see. Miss Rosemary can come back in his place."

Gus stirred uneasily. "What would ye do for clothing? We've no' the coin—"

"You're right. I've been thinking about it. I believe if I ask Cissy Standish for the loan of some garments, she'll agree. I'll make a bundle of them and take it with me."

"But—" Gus looked aghast. "Ye'll be on your own till the next stage. Where?"

"I thought I wouldn't go any farther than Cheyenne. That will alleviate the cost."

"Where will ye stay?"

"I'll find a place. Trust me, Angus. I'm tougher than I look."

"Ye're tougher than old boots, ye are."

"I hope that's a compliment."

"It is, indeed."

"So, it's a plan. I'll speak with Cissy Standish in the morning. That means there's only one thing you need to tell me. Angus." She leaned toward him and engaged his eyes. "Do you want me to return as Rosemary Fortune?"

For an instant, she saw refusal in his eyes, and her whole world tilted. If Angus changed his mind, if this man rejected her, she didn't know what she'd do. Dry up and blow away, quite possibly.

He swallowed so his Adam's apple moved up and down. But he didn't speak.

Was that her answer? Must she pack up her miserably few belongings, haul on what was left of her pride, and go?

Abruptly, his gaze softened. Very gently, he reached out and cupped her cheek.

"Lass, of course I want ye to return."

"You want me here with you?"

"I want ye here with me."

Seizing his hand in both of hers, she whispered, "Then prove it." And she towed him to the bed.

Chapter Twenty-Four

Gus stood with his hands stuffed deep in the pockets of his trousers and his coat tail flying in the wind, waiting for the stage to arrive.

Two days had passed since he'd loaded Phil onto the outgoing stage, his heart grieving so he could barely speak.

He'd put around town that his young cousin had to leave—had dropped it in the ear of everyone he met, including Buck Standish at the livery. He'd also mentioned another relation would be coming, a young lady named Rosemary.

Of course, he suspected Buck knew the truth, for he hadn't looked surprised. No doubt his wife, Cissy, had told him everything.

Which would just make it all the more humiliating if Rosemary didn't turn up on this stage. Or the next.

Or at all.

What if something had happened to her in Cheyenne? She'd meant to write her mother a letter and send it from there. What if her ma had wired her the money to come home instead?

What if, with distance and clarity, she'd realized she wanted no part of a dirt-poor undertaker in a patched, purple hat?

He wouldn't blame her. No, indeed he would not. But och, how his heart would break.

With half an eye, he watched a crew of men putting up a banner across Old Cheyenne Road. A similar banner had already gone up outside Wylder's Mercantile. *Founder's Day! Games, contests, dance.*

Dance.

His mind began spinning a fantasy. Rosemary, clad in a pretty dress and looking like the flower she was, on his arm. Her hair piled atop her head, maybe with some of those fancy combs women liked to wear. They'd attend the dance together just like a regular couple, and everyone would see the way she looked at him—not like a poor undertaker, but like the man who lit her world.

For once, he would have something of his own.

His heart yearned for it. But, as he'd learned long ago beneath old Silas's tutelage, such dreams rarely came true. Better for him to discipline his rather wild emotions and give no outward sign. Life seldom smiled upon him. He had no reason to believe, when the stage pulled in, Rosemary Fortune would be on it. Because yes, sanity might have set in, and she may have changed her mind.

"Mr. Wright? Mr. Wright!"

He turned to see Mr. Cranston hurrying up. The man looked even shabbier than he had only a couple weeks ago, his coat worn through at the elbows and his shirt tail flying. He didn't have his string of chil'ren with him this time, just the eldest boy, who followed him dutifully.

Gus gave one of his polite bows. "Mr. Cranston."

"Just the man I wanted to see." Reaching Gus, John Cranston dug in his pocket. "I have some of what I owe you. For Betsy's beautiful coffin. Not all of it, mind, not yet. But I'd like to pay you what I can."

Cranston held out his hand. Startled, Gus accepted the coins on his palm.

"I bet you thought you'd never see that," Cranston said. "But," he nodded at the lad beside him, "I mean to teach my chil'ren a debt is a debt and honor is honor. I'll have the rest of that for you, by and by. I'm only sorry it's takin' me so long."

"Thank you very much, Mr. Cranston."

"Yes, sir. I'll be forever grateful you and your young lad gave my Betsy the kind of send-off she deserved."

Unexpected tears flooded Gus's eyes and stopped his throat so he couldn't reply. Perhaps what he did, here in Wylder, was important after all.

He nodded and clasped Cranston's hand harder.

Not till the man and his son walked away did he realize the stage bore down on him.

Well, if Rosemary was in that vehicle, at least he wouldn't be meeting her completely penniless.

Dust rose in a cloud as the stage came to a halt. The driver and guard leaped down. Gus jingled the coins in his pocket as the driver came round to the door. No faces peered out the window.

His heart sank.

Maybe, he thought desperately, there would be no Founder's Day dance with Rosemary on his arm. Maybe he'd never see her again.

The door creaked when the driver hauled it open and fitted the steps into place. The weary horses lowered their heads. Nobody exited the coach.

Ah, hell. Gus had known a lot of pain in his time. The parting from his ma had devastated him. He'd cried

166

in his narrow berth, halfway across the ocean, but he'd endured. And life under Groat—that had required a fortitude he'd not imagined he possessed. He'd endured that also.

Could he endure this?

A man emerged from the coach. He carried a large satchel and looked like a salesman. When he alit, he turned back and held out his hand to someone else.

She descended from the coach like a queen, every inch of her poised and composed. She wore a dusty gray gown and a little hat to match, that sat cocked on her head. Just as he'd imagined, her dark curls, upswept, gleamed in the sunlight.

She looked too beautiful for words.

The salesman helped her down and bowed, as seemed fitting. The stage driver pulled down a bag—where had she got that, when she didn't own anything?—and she turned. Her deep blue eyes found Gus, and fastened upon him.

His relief overwhelming, he couldn't move. This splendid creature could not possibly be here for him. Yet she smiled and stretched out her hands.

"Cousin Angus? It's been so long!"

Gus's relief staggered him. He wanted to embrace her. Would long-lost relations do that? But a few people, curious, turned their heads, so he merely caught her hands in his.

"Cousin Rosemary."

She squeezed his fingers hard. Her gaze seemed to move over his face and consume him.

He gave another of his bows. "How was your journey?"

"Long and arduous. Those are some rough roads, I

tell you. I am surprised we are not late."

"You are a bit late." *I feared you would not come.*

"I'll admit, I was desperate to arrive."

Gus thumbed over, in his mind, what they'd agreed to say. "How are your parents? And—and the rest of the family."

"Mother is the same as ever. She made me promise I'd write. Father is a martyr to his rheumatism."

"I'm sorry to hear it."

She took his arm and pressed close, so close he could feel the heat of her body. He trembled within.

"So, show me this grand shop of yours."

"It is no' grand."

"No?" She turned and looked at him, gazing deep into his eyes. "Then we will make it so. Together, yes?"

They paused in the middle of the dusty street. Folks hurried around them, and behind Gus the stage driver finished unloading the last of the baggage.

Gus whispered, "I can't believe ye came back."

She lifted elegant brows. "Wasn't that the plan?"

"Aye. Aye."

"I have such news! Let's get somewhere we can speak privately."

"Braw news, is it?"

"Very braw indeed. Besides," she whispered, "I desperately need to kiss you, and I can scarcely do that here in the open, can I?"

Gus's heart bounded. "No, indeed."

"Then let's go home, Angus."

Home.

Chapter Twenty-Five

Phoebe wondered about the tentative look in Angus's eyes. She'd learned to read the man the way a sea captain read the ocean. His face might not give away much, but that soulful gaze told a story.

Something continued to bother him. Even though she had his arm clutched firmly in hers, and though her heart danced with gladness at being with him again, he held back.

The time away from him had seemed endless, and had taught her a few important truths. She didn't think she could live without this man. She didn't want to try.

When they entered the shop, she paused and inhaled a deep breath of sawdust mixed with the other scents that made up the place.

Then she looked at Angus. "Is Ned at school?"

"He is. He—"

She let him get no farther before lifting onto her tiptoes and pressing her mouth to his.

Bliss ensued, the kind that made a woman's toes curl inside her slippers and sent all the worry floating away. So strong were the feelings, it took her several moments to realize that though yes, Angus participated, he still held back.

She ended the kiss and gazed at him. So focused had she been on getting back to him, and with good news, she'd never paused to doubt her welcome.

Until now.

"Angus? What is it?" If he'd changed his mind while she was away, if he'd decided he didn't want her crashing back into his life after all—well, that very thought had the floor dropping away beneath her feet, and made it hard to breathe.

She pressed one hand to her chest.

He shook his head and his gaze fled hers. "Ye looked so grand, stepping down from that coach."

"Grand? Me?"

"Aye."

"Don't be fooled. I'm still the ragged lad who ran around the place barefoot, half covered in paint." And lost all hope of decorum, in his bed.

That won her a smile. "I'm glad," he said.

Would he not say he'd missed her, the way she'd missed him, with every beat of her heart? Oh, being in love was risky. No wonder she'd spent her life up till now avoiding it.

She turned away, took off her—Cissy's—hat and laid it on the table before stealing another look at him. "Are you not glad to see me?" Perhaps, him being a man, she needed to ask it outright.

"Och, aye."

"Well, something is clearly amiss. And we are going to have it out here and now, Angus Wright. For, if we're to have a proper relationship, there will be no secrets between us and no misunderstandings, great or small."

He searched her face. "Are we? To have a proper relationship?"

Her heart fell. "That's why I returned. But—but," her lips grew stiff over the words, "if you don't want me here—"

He closed his eyes for a moment, like a man in pain. "I thought once ye got awa' from here, clear o' all the—the madness and the—"

"Passion?"

"Aye, the passion, and had a chance to think on it, you'd change your mind. Decide ye didn't want a life here in Wylder with a low-class undertaker who has nothing to recommend him."

"You thought that, did you?"

"I did. I did. I stood there waiting for that stage, thinking ye would not be on it, and when ye got off, why—ye looked so much the lady, I knew ye could not be for me."

Heavens! He became downright near unintelligible when agitated. Yet her heart rose, bounding like a bird on the wing.

"Then, why do you suppose I did return?"

He shook his head again. "I do no' ken."

"Angus, I've left my old life behind. I've written to my mother, told her Phoebe Corbet is buried. That's my choice. I invited her to make her own choice and come out here to join me if she will.

"I want a life with you, here. I want the warmth, the companionship—the laughter we share. But if you have doubts, if you've changed your mind about wanting me, well—" Her heart thudded. "Say so now. And I'll leave on the next conveyance out of town."

He swallowed convulsively. "Of course I want ye, lass. But it seems I've so little to offer ye. Look around this place. I've no' a home to speak of and barely the means to put food on the table."

"And who says you're the only one who can

provide?"

"A man provides for the woman he…loves."

Phoebe went silent a moment on gladness so sharp it made her ache. If he loved her, nothing else mattered.

"Look at this." She let go of him and turned to her bag, which she'd set down on the floor when they came in. She withdrew a purse, and from it swiftly poured coins into his hands. His expression altered to one of amazement.

"There, Angus, can we live on this for a time? In addition to what we earn, of course. I want to keep working—working with you."

"What have ye done? Robbed a bank?"

"Why would I need to, when I already stole a small fortune in jewels?"

"Aye, but the jewels were lost."

"Only, they weren't. When I went to the post office in Cheyenne to mail my letter to Mother, there was a parcel waiting for me. This parcel." She scrabbled for it, inside the bag. Wrapped in brown paper, and bound with string all too obviously retied, it bulged at the sides.

On the front it read, *Miss Phoebe Corbet, c/o the Cheyenne Post Office*, in awkward lettering.

Angus appeared floored. "Ye got this at the post office?"

"I did."

"But—how did ye know it was there?"

"I didn't. I just went to the post office hoping Mother might have sent a letter. I thought she might know what's happened to Emil. When the postal clerk checked, there was no letter for a Phoebe Corbet, but there was this package."

With hands that trembled slightly, she untied the string. Even in the low light of the tiny room, the jewels within caught a gleam. A flash from a ruby, a sapphire. A glint of gold.

Gus gasped. "That's—"

"My jewelry, yes. Or rather, half of it." Phoebe grinned. "Emil took the rest. He enclosed a note. See? He wrote only three words. *I am sorry.*"

Gus blinked in astonishment. "He's alive? He stole from you?"

"Seems that way, doesn't it?" Phoebe's heart tripped, double time. She'd trusted Emil implicitly. Just went to show how risky it was, placing trust in any man.

But this man—Angus Wright—he was different. And that—that was why she'd returned. She could trust him with everything she had, everything she was. Even with her heart.

Now, though, he fired up. "Emil slipped out on you? After nailing you inside that casket? What if ye couldn't get out? You might have died."

"No doubt that's why he left half the haul, out of guilt. And yes, I might have died, had it not been for you." She slid her hands up the shoulders of his coat. "You saved me." In more ways than one. He'd become her place to belong.

And oh, she wanted to be his!

She framed his face with her hands. "Angus, don't you see? I've only sold a fraction of that jewelry and already I've got—well, a fortune. We can enlarge the shop. We can build a house and provide for both Ned and Mother when she comes. You can buy a horse and wagon, or even a hearse."

"If—if you wish to share all that wi' me."

"What else would I want? I have only one question for you, Angus Wright. After all that's passed between us, how could you even imagine I wouldn't want to return to you?"

His eyes met hers, and in them she saw his doubt and hope, the kindness that characterized him. She saw the man he was, and the beauty of his spirit stole her breath away.

"I confess, Phoebe, when I mentioned marriage and ye rejected the idea so heartily, I had trouble believing ye truly did wish to be wi' me."

She lifted a brow. "Marriage? Is that what this is all about? Angus, you have to understand. Jasper's treatment of Mother showed me the worst of that state. I'm not eager to jump into it. Wouldn't you rather I chose every day to be with you? Isn't it better I should stay willingly, rather than because I'm sworn to?"

"If you truly will make that choice every day."

"I will." She leaned up and whispered it against his lips. "I will."

How could she convince him? "I know. Come look at this." She towed him by the hand back out into the workshop. Once there, she plowed through a stack of lumber against the rear wall.

"This was meant to be a surprise," she told him, drawing out a large plank.

She'd done her very best work on this, in the moments he was away. And she'd managed to complete it right before she left for Cheyenne.

She'd painted the background white. Against it, a pattern of leaves stood out in stark relief—green leaves for the living, transitioning in an arc to leaves brown and sere.

The lettering also curved, reading *Wright and Fortune. Quality coffins, Signage, Murals.*

"Murals?" Gus asked, spelling it out.

"I didn't mention it, but Mr. Wylder at the mercantile was asking about that. Don't you see, Angus? We can have a life, a good one, and my ill-gotten gains can give us a leg up."

"I see."

"The point is, would I have made this sign if I didn't intend to return to you?"

"I reckon not."

"Neither do I. So, Angus Wright, if you're willing to cast your fortune in with mine, I'll be very content to declare I've found the *wright* man."

Light took hold in his eyes. "Yes, ma'am. I'm willing."

"Then there's just one more thing to be said."

"What's that?"

"Take off your hat."

"My hat? Why?"

"Because I know you set great store by it, and I'm about to kiss you so hard it's bound to be knocked right off."

One of his spectacular smiles broke across his face. He snatched the top hat from his hair and tossed it atop the nearest coffin.

"Aye, Rosemary Fortune. That's an undertaking in which I'm more than willing to participate."

A word about the author...

Multi-award-winning author Laura Strickland delights in time traveling to the past and searching out settings for her books, be they Historical Romance, Steampunk or something in between. Her first Scottish Historical hero, *Devil Black*, battled his way onto the publishing scene in 2013, and the author never looked back.

Nor has she yet tapped the limits of her imagination. Venturing beyond Historical and Contemporary Romance, she created a new world with her ground-breaking Buffalo Steampunk Adventure series set in her native city in Western New York.

Married and the parent of one grown daughter, Laura has also been privileged to mother a number of very special rescue dogs, and is intensely interested in animal welfare. These days while she's writing, you can always find her latest rescue, Lacy, nearby. Her love of dogs, and her lifelong interest in Celtic history, magic and music, are all reflected in her writing. Laura's mantra is Lore, Legend, Love, and she wouldn't have it any other way.

www.ingramcontent.com/pod-product-compliance
Lightning Source LLC
Chambersburg PA
CBHW061136200626
46817CB00016B/1660